*Praise fo*

# Diving Belles

*from abroad*

Longlisted for the
Frank O'Connor International Short Story Award

"Magical and bewitching tales." — *Vogue*

"Wood's finely wrought collection has touches of a benign Angela Carter and recalls the playful yet political transmogrifications of Atwood and Byatt." — *Guardian*

"Bewitching . . . Centered mostly around women—young women, old women, women becalmed somewhere in between—magic encroaches upon their narratives as slowly but surely as the incoming tide." — *Daily Mail*

"Winsome, quirky, and sometimes enchanting, Wood's stories seem to fish about in rock pools of imagination." — *Sunday Times*

"Wood's imagination is extraordinary; she has an instinct for the inner meanings of myths that echoes the great Angela Carter. Superb." — *Times*

"Beautiful, spooky." — *Harper's Bazaar*

# DIVING BELLES

# DIVING BELLES

## and Other Stories

## Lucy Wood

Mariner Books
Houghton Mifflin Harcourt
*Boston   New York*

First Mariner Books edition 2012
Copyright © 2012 by Lucy Wood

For information about permission to reproduce selections from this
book, write to Permissions, Houghton Mifflin Harcourt Publishing
Company, 215 Park Avenue South, New York, New York 10003.

www.hmhbooks.com

First published in Great Britain by Bloomsbury Publishing in 2012


*Library of Congress Cataloging-in-Publication Data*
Wood, Lucy.
Diving belles and other stories / Lucy Wood. — 1st Mariner Books ed.
p. cm.
ISBN 978-0-547-59553-5
1. Title.
PR6123.O4727D59 2012
823'.92 — DC23
2012014406


Printed in the United States of America
DOC 10 9 8 7 6 5 4 3 2 1

For Mum and Dad

# Contents

# Diving Belles

Iris crossed her brittle ankles and folded her hands in her lap as the diving bell creaked and juddered towards the sea. At first, she could hear Demelza shouting and cursing as she cranked the winch, but as the bell was cantilevered away from the deck her voice was lost in the wind. Cold air rushed through the open bottom of the bell, bringing with it the rusty smell of *The Matriarch*'s liver-spotted flanks and the brackish damp of seaweed. The bench Iris was sitting on was narrow and every time the diving bell rocked she pressed against the footrest to steady herself. She kept imagining that she was inside a church bell and that she was the clapper about to ring out loudly into the water, announcing something. She fixed her eyes on the small window and didn't look down. There was no floor beneath her feet, just a wide open gap, and the sea peaked and spat. She lurched downwards slowly, metres away from the side of the trawler, where a layer of barnacles and mussels clung on like the survivors of a shipwreck.

She fretted with her new dress and her borrowed shoes. She tried to smooth her white hair, which turned wiry when it was close to water. The wooden bench was digging into her and the wind was rushing up her legs, snagging at the dress and exposing the map of her veins. She'd forgotten tights; she always wore trousers and knew it was a mistake to wear a dress. She'd let herself get talked into it, but had chosen brown, a small victory. She gathered the skirt up and sat on it. If this was going to be the first time she saw her husband in forty-eight years she didn't want to draw attention to the state of her legs. 'You've got to be heartbreaking as hell,' Demelza advised her customers, pointing at them with her cigarette. 'Because you've got a lot of competition down there.'

Salt and spray leapt up to meet the bell as it slapped into the sea. Cold, dark water surged upwards. Iris lifted her feet, waiting for the air pressure in the bell to level off the water underneath the footrest. She didn't want anything oily or foamy to stain Annie's shoes. She went through a checklist – Vanish, cream cleaner, a bit of bicarb – something would get it out but it would be a fuss. She pulled her cardigan sleeves down and straightened the life-jacket. Thousands of bubbles forced themselves up the sides of the diving bell, rolling over the window like marbles. She peered out but couldn't see anything beyond the disturbed water.

As she was lowered further the sea calmed and stilled. Everything was silent. She put her feet back down and looked into the disc of water below them, which was flat and thick and barely rippled. She could be looking at a lino or slate floor rather than a gap that opened into all those airless fathoms. A smudged grey shape floated past. The diving bell jolted and tipped, then righted itself and sank lower through the water.

Iris held her handbag against her chest and tried not to breathe too quickly. She had about two hours' worth of oxygen but if she panicked or became over-excited she would use it up more quickly. Her fingers laced and unlaced. 'I don't want to have to haul you back up here like a limp fish,' Demelza had told her each time she'd gone down in the bell. 'Don't go thinking you're an expert or anything. One pull on the cord to stop, another to start again. Two tugs for the net and three to come back up. Got it?' Iris had written the instructions down the first time in her thin, messy writing and put them in her bag along with tissues and mints, just in case. The pull-cord was threaded through a tube that ran alongside the chain attaching the bell to the trawler. Demelza tied her end of it to a cymbal that she'd rigged on to a tripod, so that it crashed loudly whenever someone pulled on it. The other end of the cord drooped down and brushed roughly against the top of Iris's head.

She couldn't see much out of the window; it all looked grey and endless, as if she were moving through fog rather than water. The diving bell dropped down slowly, slower, and then stopped moving altogether. The chain slackened and for a second it seemed as though the bell had been cut off and was about to float away. Then the chain straightened out and Iris rocked sideways, caught between the tension above and the bell's heavy lead rim below. She hung suspended in the mid-depths of the sea. This had happened on her second dive as well. Demelza had suddenly stopped winching, locked the handle and gone to check over her co-ordinates one last time. She wouldn't allow the diving bell to land even a foot off the target she'd set herself.

The bell swayed. Iris sat very still and tried not to imagine the weight of the water pressing in. She took a couple of rattling breaths. It was like those moments when she woke up in the middle of the night, breathless and alone, reaching across the bed and finding nothing but a heap of night-chilled pillows. She just needed to relax and wait, relax and wait. She took out a mint and crunched down hard, the grainy sugar digging into her back teeth.

After a few moments Demelza started winching again and Iris loosened her shoulders, glad to be on the move. Closer to the seabed, the water seemed to clear. Then, suddenly, there was the shipwreck, looming upwards like an unlit bonfire, all splints and beams and slumped funnels. The rusting mainframe arched and jutted. Collapsed sheets of iron were strewn across the sand. The diving bell moved between girders and cables before stopping just above the engine. The *Queen Mary*'s sign, corroded and nibbled, gazed up at Iris. Empty cupboards were scattered to her left. The cargo ship had been transporting train carriages and they were lying all over the seabed, marooned and broken, like bodies that had been weighed down with stones and buried at sea. Orange rust bloomed all over them. Green and purple seaweed drifted out through the windows. Red man's fingers and dead man's fingers pushed up from the wheel arches.

Demelza thought that this would be a good place to trawl. She'd sent Iris down to the same spot already. 'Sooner or later,' she said, 'they all come back. They stay local, you see. They might go gallivanting off for a while, but they always come back to the same spot. They're nostalgic bastards, sentimental as hell. That makes them stupid. Not like us though, eh?' she added, yanking Iris's life-jacket straps tighter.

A cuckoo wrasse weaved in and out of the ship's bones. Cuttlefish mooned about like lost old men. Iris spat on her glasses, wiped them on her cardigan, hooked them over her ears, and waited.

\*    \*    \*

4

Over the years, she had tried to banish as many lonely moments as possible. She kept busy. She took as many shifts as she could at the hotel, and then when that stopped she became addicted to car boot sales – travelling round to different ones at the weekends, sifting through chipped plates and dolls and candelabra, never buying anything, just sifting through. She joined a pen pal company and started writing to a man in Orkney; she liked hearing about the sudden weather and the seals hauled out on the beach, his bus and his paintings. 'I am fine as always,' she would write, but stopped when he began to send dark, tormented paintings, faces almost hidden under black and red.

She knew how to keep busy most of the day and, over time, her body learned to shut down and nap during the blank gap straight after lunch. It worked almost every time, although once, unable to sleep and sick of the quiet humming of the freezer – worse than silence she often thought – she turned it off and let the food melt and drip on the floor. Later, regretting the waste, she'd spent hours cooking, turning it into pies and casseroles and refreezing it for another day.

She ate in front of films she borrowed from the library. She watched anything she could get her hands on. It was when the final credits rolled, though, when the music had stopped and the tape rewound, that her mind became treacherous and leapt towards the things she tried not to think about during the day. That was when she lay back in the chair – kicking and jolting between wakefulness and sleep as if she were thrashing about in shallow water – and let her husband swim back into the house.

Then, she relived the morning when she had woken to the smell of salt and damp and found a tiny fish in its death throes on the pillow next to her. There was only a lukewarm indent in the mattress where her husband should have been. She swung her legs out of bed and followed a trail of sand down the stairs, through the kitchen and towards the door. Her heart thumped in the soles of her bare feet. The door was open. Two green crabs high-stepped across the slates. Bladderwrack festooned the kitchen, and here and there, on the fridge, on the kettle, anemones bloomed, fat and dark as hearts. It took her all day to scrub and bleach and mop the house back into shape. By the time she'd finished he could have been anywhere. She didn't phone the police; no one ever phoned the police. No one was reported missing.

Despite the bleach, the smell lingered in cupboards and corners. Every so often, an anemone would appear overnight; she would find a translucent shrimp darting around inside an empty milk bottle. Sometimes, all the water in the house turned into brine and she lugged huge bottles of water home from the supermarket. The silence waxed and waned. Life bedded itself down again like a hermit crab in a bigger, emptier shell.

Once in a while, Annie and her husband Westy came round to see Iris. They lived on the same street and came over when Annie had something she wanted to say or if she was bored. She could smell out bad news and liked to talk about it, her own included. Westy went wherever she went. He was a vague man. He'd got his whole Scout group lost when he was twelve because he'd read the compass wrong, so he was nicknamed Westy and it stuck – everyone used it, even his wife; sometimes Iris wondered if he could even remember his real name. When Annie dies, she sometimes thought, his mind will go, just like that, and mentally she would snap her fingers, instantly regretting thinking it.

When she heard them coming up the path she would rush

round the house, checking water filters, tearing thrift off the shelves. If she ever missed something, a limpet shell, a watery cluster of sea moss, Annie and Westy would look away, pretending not to notice.

Last month, they came over on a Sunday afternoon. 'I don't like Sundays,' Annie said, drinking her tea at scalding point. 'They make me feel like I'm in limbo.' She was short and spread herself out over the chair. She made Iris want to stoop over.

It was damp outside and the kitchen windows had steamed up. Annie had brought over saffron cake and Iris bit at the edges, feeling she had to but hating the chlorine taste of it. She'd told Annie that before but she kept bringing it over anyway.

'Don't forget the envelope,' Westy said.

Annie shot him a quick look. 'I'll come to that.' She glanced down at her bag. 'Have you heard about the burglaries around King's Road?'

'I read something about it,' Iris said. She crossed her arms, knowing that Annie was trying to ease into something.

'Five over two weeks. All in the middle of the day. The owners came back to stripped houses – everything gone, even library books.'

'Library books?' Iris said. She saw that Annie and Westy were wearing the same fleece in different colours – one purple, one checked red and green.

'Exactly. One of the owners said they saw a van driving away. They saw the men in there looking at them.' Annie paused, looked at Westy. 'Imagine going in there, seeing the bare walls, knowing that someone had gone through everything, valuing it.'

'Their shoes,' Westy said.

'Everything,' said Annie. 'And no chance of ever getting it back.' She stopped, waiting for Iris to speak, but Iris didn't say anything.

Annie reached down into her bag and got out a blue and gold envelope and put it on the table, cleared her throat. 'Ever heard of Diving Belles?' she asked bluntly.

Iris didn't look at the envelope. 'I suppose so,' she said. She saw Annie take a deep breath – she was bad at this, had never liked giving out gifts. Iris's mind raced through ways she could steer the conversation away; she snatched at topics but couldn't fasten on to any.

'When Kayleigh Andrews did it,' Annie told her, 'it only took one go. They found her husband as quick as anything.'

Iris didn't reply. She tightened her lips and poured out more tea.

'It seems like a very lucrative business,' Annie said, pressing on. 'A good opportunity.'

'Down on the harbour,' said Westy. 'By the old lifeboat hut.'

Iris knocked crumbs into her cupped palm from the table edge and tipped them into her saucer. The clock on the fridge ticked loudly into the silence. The old anger swept back. She could break all these plates.

'A good opportunity,' Annie said again.

'For some people,' Iris replied. A fly buzzed over and she banged a plate down hard on to it.

'What you need is one of those electric swatters,' Westy told her.

'You shouldn't have gone to the trouble,' Iris said. She gripped the sides of her chair.

Annie pushed the envelope so it was right in front of her. 'The voucher's redeemable for three goes,' she said.

'It's kind of you.'

They looked around the room as if they had never seen it before, the cream walls and brown speckled tiles. A sea snail crawled over the window-sill.

'I can't swim. I won't be able to do it if I can't swim,' Iris said suddenly.

'You don't need to swim. You just sit in this bell thing and get lowered down,' Annie said. 'The voucher gives you three goes, Iris. You don't have to swim anywhere.'

Iris stood up, stacked the cups and plates, and took them to the sink. Soon Annie would say something like, 'Nothing ventured, nothing gained.' Her hands trembled slightly, the crockery clattering together like pebbles flipping over.

After they'd left, she watched the envelope out of the corner of her eye. She did small jobs that took her closer towards it: she swept the floor, straightened the chairs, the tablecloth. Later, lying in bed, she pictured it sitting there. It was very exposed in the middle of the table like that – what if somebody broke in? It would be a waste of Annie's money if the voucher was stolen. She went downstairs, picked up the envelope, brought it back upstairs and tucked it under her pillow.

The reception at Diving Belles was in an old corrugated-iron Portakabin on the edge of the harbour. Iris knocked tentatively on the door. The wind hauled itself around the town, crashing into bins and slumping into washing, jangling the rigging on the fishing boats. There were piles of nets and lobster pots and orange buoys that smelled of fish and stagnant water. No one answered the door. She stepped back to check she had the right place, then knocked again. There was a clanging above her head as a woman walked across the roof. She was wearing khaki trousers, a tight black vest and jelly shoes. Her hair was short and dyed red. She climbed down a ladder and stood in front of Iris, staring. Her hands were criss-crossed with scars and her broad shoulders and arms were covered in tattoos. Iris couldn't take her eyes off them. She watched an eel swim through a hollow black heart on the woman's bicep.

'Is it, I mean, are you Demelza?' Iris asked.

'Demelza, Demelza . . . Yes, I suppose I am.' Demelza looked up at the roof and stepped back as if to admire something. There was a strange contraption up there – it looked like a metal cage with lots of thick springs. 'That ought to do it,' Demelza muttered to herself.

Iris looked up. Was that a seagull sprawled inside or a plastic bag?

Demelza strode off towards the office without saying anything else. Iris hesitated, then followed her.

The office smelled like old maps and burnt coffee. Demelza sat behind a desk which had a hunting knife skewered into one corner. Iris perched on the edge of a musty deckchair. Paperwork and files mixed with rusty boat parts. There was a board on the wall with hundreds of glinting turquoise and silver scales pinned to it.

Demelza leaned back in her chair and lit a cigarette. 'These are herbal,' she said. 'Every drag is like death.' She inhaled deeply then rubbed at her knuckles, rocking back and forth on the chair's back legs.

Iris tensed her back, trying to keep straight so that her deckchair wouldn't collapse. The slats creaked. She felt too warm even though the room was cold.

'So,' Demelza barked suddenly. 'What are we dealing with here? Husband taken?'

Iris nodded.

Demelza rummaged around in the desk drawer and pulled out a form. 'How many nights ago?'

'I'm not exactly sure.'

'Spit it out. Three? Seven? If you haven't counted the nights I don't know why you're pestering me about it.'

'Seventeen thousand, six hundred and thirty-two,' Iris said.

'What the hell? There's not room for that on this form.' Demelza looked at her. Her eyes were slightly bloodshot and she didn't seem to blink.

'If it doesn't fit on the form then don't trouble yourself,' Iris said. She started to get up, relief and disappointment merging.

'Hang on, hang on.' Demelza gestured for her to sit back down. 'I didn't say I wouldn't do it. It makes more sense anyway now I come to think about it. I've never known them to be bothered by an old codger before.' She sniggered to herself.

'He was twenty-four.'

'Exactly, exactly.' Demelza scribbled something down on the form. 'But this is going to be damn tricky, you know. There's a chance he will have migrated; he could have been abandoned; he could be anywhere. You understand that?' Iris nodded again. 'Good. I need you to sign here – just a simple legal clause about safety and the like, and to confirm you know that I'm not legally obliged to produce the husband. If I can't find him it's tough titties, OK?'

Iris signed it.

'And how I track them is business secrets,' Demelza said. 'Don't bother asking me about it. I don't want competition.'

A plastic singing fish leered down at Iris from the wall. She could feel tendrils of her hair slipping from behind their pins. She always wore her hair up, but once she'd left it down and nobody in her local shop had recognised her. When she'd ventured back she'd had to pretend that she'd been away for a while. She dug a pin in deeper. Was Demelza smirking at her? She hunched down in the chair, almost wishing it would fold up around her. She shouldn't have come. She waited for Demelza to say something but she was just rocking back and forth, one leg draped over the desk.

'The weather's warming up,' Iris said eventually, although it was colder than ever.

Demelza said something through her teeth about seagulls and tourists then sighed and stood up. 'Come on,' she said. They walked to the end of the harbour. Small waves lifted up handfuls of seaweed at the bottom of the harbour wall. Demelza pointed to an old beam trawler. 'There she is.'

'There she is,' Iris said. *The Matriarch* was yellow and haggard as an old fingernail. Rust curled off the bottom. It looked like it was struggling to stay afloat. Its figurehead was a decapitated mermaid and the deck smelled of tar and sewage. None of the other boats had anchored near it.

Demelza took a deep sniff. 'Beautiful, isn't she?' Without waiting for an answer she walked up the ramp and on to the boat. The diving bell was sitting on a platform next to the wheel. It looked ancient and heavy, like a piece of armour. For the first time, Iris realised she'd be going right under the sea. Picturing herself inside, she remembered a pale bird she had once seen hanging in a cage in a shop window.

Demelza ran her hand across the metal. She explained how the diving bell worked. 'See, when it's submerged the air and the water pressure balance so the water won't come in past the bench. The oxygen gets trapped in the top. Of course, modern ones do it differently; there are pipes and things that pump oxygen down from the boat. Apparently that's "safer". They have all this crap like phones in there but they're not as beautiful as this one. This one is a real beauty. Why would you need a goddamn phone under the sea?' She looked at Iris as if she expected an answer.

Iris thought about comfort and calling for help. 'Well,' she said. 'No one likes change, do they?'

Demelza clapped her hard on the back. 'My sentiment exactly.' They walked back along the harbour. 'Give me a few days to track any signs then I'll give you a buzz,' she said.

Fifteen minutes passed inside the diving bell. It could have been seconds or hours. The bulk of the *Queen Mary* was dark and still. Iris noticed every small movement. A spider crab poked its head out of a hole. A sea slug pulsed across the keel. The seaweed swayed and rocked in small currents and, following them with her eyes, Iris rocked into a thin sleep, then jolted awake with a gasp, thinking she had fallen into the water, feeling herself hit the cold and start to sink. She hadn't slept well the night before but it was ridiculous and dangerous to fall asleep here, to come all this way and sleep. She pinched her wrist and shifted on the bench, wishing Demelza had put some sort of cushion on it.

Time passed. A ray swam up and pasted itself to the glass like a wet leaf. It had a small, angry face. Its mouth gaped. The diving bell became even darker inside and Iris couldn't see anything out of the window. 'Get away,' she said. Nothing happened. She leaned forwards and banged hard on the glass until the ray unpeeled itself and disappeared. Her heart beat fast and heavy. Every time she glimpsed a fish darting, or saw a small shadow, she thought that it was him swimming towards her. She worked herself up and then nothing happened. Her heart slowed down again.

Demelza was sure there would be a sighting. She said that she'd recorded a lot more movement around the wreck in the past few days, but to Iris it seemed as empty and lonely as ever.

Something caught her eye and she half stood on the footrest to look out. Nothing – probably seaweed. Her knees shook, not up to the task of hefting her about in such a narrow gap. She sat back down. Even if he did appear, even if she made him follow the diving bell until Demelza could reach him with the net, what would she say to him on deck? What was that phrase Annie had picked up? 'Long time no see'? She practised saying it. 'Long time no see.' It sounded odd and caught in her throat. She cleared it and tried again. 'Actually, long time lots of sea,' she joked into the hollow metal. It fell flat. She thought of all the things she wanted to tell him. There were so many things but none of them were right. They stacked up in front of her like bricks, dense and dry. She had a sudden thought and colour seeped up her neck and into her cheeks. Of course, he was going to be naked. She had forgotten about that. She'd be standing there, thinking of something to say, and Demelza would be there, and he'd be naked. It had been so long since . . . She didn't know whether she would . . . Was she a wife or a stranger? She picked at the fragile skin around her nails, tearing it to pieces.

On the first dive, Iris had got a sense of how big it all was, how vast; emptier and more echoing than she had thought possible. It made her feel giddy and sick. She had presumed that there would be something here – she didn't know what – but she hadn't imagined this nothingness stretching on and on. She shuddered, hating the cold and the murk, regretting ever picking up the envelope from the table. The silence bothered her. She didn't like to think of him somewhere so silent.

As she went deeper, small memories rose up to meet her. A fine net of flour over his dark hair; a song on his lips that went, 'My old man was a sailor, I saw him once a year'; a bee, but she didn't know what the bee was connected to.

She saw something up ahead: a small, dark shape swimming towards her. Her stomach lurched. It had to be him – he had sensed her and was coming to meet her! She pulled on the cord, once, hard, to stop. The bell drifted down for a few moments then lurched to a halt. Iris craned her neck forwards, trying to make him out properly. She should have done this years ago.

He came closer, swimming with his arms behind him. What colour was that? His skin looked very dark; a kind of red-brown. He swam closer and her heart dropped down into her feet. It was an octopus. Its curled legs drifted out behind as it swam around the bell, its body like a bag snagged on a tree. She had thought this octopus was her husband! Shame and a sudden tiredness coursed through her. She tried to laugh but only the smallest corner of her mouth twitched, then wouldn't stop. 'You silly fool,' she told herself. 'You silly fool.' She watched its greedy eyes inspecting the bell, then pulled three times on the cord. A spasm of weariness gripped her. She told Demelza she hadn't seen anything.

'I thought you had, when you wanted to stop suddenly,' Demelza said. She took a swig from a hip flask and offered it to Iris, who sipped until her dry lips burned. 'Wouldn't have thought they'd have been mid-water like that, but still, they can be wily bastards at times.' She turned round and squinted at Iris, who was sitting very quietly with her eyes closed. 'No sea legs,' Demelza said to herself. 'You know what the best advice I heard was?' she asked loudly. 'You can't chuck them back in once they're out.' She shook her head and bit her knuckles. 'I had a woman yesterday, a regular. She comes every couple of weeks. Her husband is susceptible to them, she says. So she goes down, we net him up and lug him back on to the deck, all pale and fat, dripping salt and seaweed like a goddamn seal. And all the time I'm thinking, what the hell's the point? Leave him down there.

But she's got it in her head that she can't live without him so that's that.'

'Maybe she loves him,' Iris said.

'Bah. There are plenty more fish in the sea,' Demelza said. She laughed and laughed, barking and cawing like a seagull. 'There are plenty more fish in the sea,' she said again, baring her teeth to the wind. 'Plenty, fish, sea,' she muttered over and over as she steered back to the harbour.

On her second dive Iris heard the beginning of a song threading through the water towards her. It was slow and deep, more of an ache in her bones than something she heard in her ears. There was a storm building up but Demelza thought it would hold off long enough to do the dive. At first Iris thought the sound was the wind, stoked right up and reaching down into the water – it was the same noise as the wind whistling through gaps in boats, or over the mouth of a milk bottle, but she knew that the wind wouldn't come down this far. It thrummed through the metal and into her bones, maybe just her old body complaining again, playing tricks, but she felt so light and warm. The song grew louder, slowing Iris's heart, pressing her eyes closed like kind thumbs. It felt good to have her eyes closed. The weight of the water pressed in but it was calm, inviting; it beckoned to her. She wanted to get out of the bell, just get up and slip through the gap at the bottom. She almost did it. She was lifting herself stiffly from the bench when the song stopped and slipped away like a cloud diffusing into the sky, leaving her cold and lonely inside the bell. Then the storm began, quietly thumping far away like someone moving boxes around in a dusty attic.

\* \* \*

16

Iris waited, shuffling and sighing. She felt tired and uncomfortable. Her last dive. She wanted tea and a hot-water bottle. It was chilly and there were too many shapes, too many movements – she couldn't keep hold of it all at once, things moved then vanished, things shifted out of sight. She was sick and tired of half glimpsing things. It had all been a waste of time. She cursed Annie for making her think there was a chance, that it wasn't all over and done with. She would give the dress away and after a while she would see somebody else walking round in it. Her glasses dug into her nose.

She felt for the cord, ready to pull it and get Demelza to haul her back up. She had never felt so old. She stretched the skin on the backs of her hands and watched it go white, and then wrinkle up into soft pouches. Her eyes were dry and itchy. She saw a flicker of something bright over to one side of the wreck. It was red, or maybe gold; she had just seen a flash. Then a large shape moved into the collapsed hollow of the ship, followed by two more shapes. There were a group of them, all hair and muscled tails and movement. They were covered in shells and kelp and their long hair was tangled and matted into dark, wet ropes. They eddied and swirled like pieces of bright, solidified water.

Then he was there. He broke away from the group and drifted through the wreck like a pale shaft of light. Iris blinked and adjusted her glasses. The twists and turns of his body – she knew it was him straight away, although there was something different, something more muscular, more streamlined and at home in the water about his body than she had ever seen. She leaned forwards and grabbed for the cord but then her throat tightened.

No one had told her he would be young. At no point had she thought he would be like this, unchanged since they'd gone to sleep that night all those years before. His skin! It was so thin, almost translucent, fragile and lovely with veins branching through him like blown ink. She had expected to see herself mirrored in him. She touched her own skin. His body moved effortlessly through the water. He was lithe, just as skinny, but more moulded, polished like a piece of sea glass.

He swam closer and she leaned back on the bench and held her breath, suddenly not wanting him to see her. She kept as still as possible, willing his eyes to slide past; they were huge and bright and more heavily lidded than she remembered. She leaned back further. He didn't look at the bell. Bubbles streamed out of his colourless mouth. He was so beautiful, so strange. She couldn't take her eyes off him.

There were spots on her glasses and she couldn't see him as well as she wanted to. She breathed on the lenses and wiped them quickly. Her hands shook and she fumbled with them, dropping them into the open water under the bench. They floated on the surface and she bent down to scoop them out but couldn't reach. Her hips creaked and locked; she couldn't reach down that far. One lens dipped into the water and then they sank completely. Iris blinked. Everything mixed together into a soft, light blur. She peered out, desperately trying to see him. He was still there. He was keeping close to the seabed, winging his way around the wreck, but every-thing about him had seeped into a smudgy paleness, like a running watercolour or an old photograph exposed to light. He was weaving in and out of the train carriages, in through a door and out through a window, threading his body through the silence and the rust. Iris tried to keep him in focus, tried to concentrate on him so that she wouldn't lose him. But she couldn't tell if he had reappeared from one of the carriages. Where was he, exactly? It was as if he were melting slowly into the sea, the water infusing his skin; his skin becoming that bit of light, that bit of movement. Iris watched and waited until she didn't know if he was there or not there, near or far away, staying or leaving.

# Countless Stones

*It is said that the stones cannot be counted;*
*they move, they shift, they come and go.*

RITA COULD FEEL it in her toes; it was always the toes first with her. They were heavier and they ached and when she reached down to touch them they felt harder and colder than usual. She moved them around in the bed but it didn't take the edge off. The middle of each toe had already turned into stone and the weight of them reminded her of the marbles she and her brother used to play with – grannies, kings, cat's eyes – so that she could almost hear the soft clicks the marbles made when they hit each other. The top layer of skin had started to dry out and soon it would harden like that brittle layer of sand that bakes and hardens on a beach. And then there was the first pang of the craving for salt that she always got when this happened.

How long did she have? About ten hours. The whole thing usually took about ten hours. It was slow, but not slow enough that she couldn't feel it if she concentrated: each skin layer seizing up and turning into stone from the inside out, a sort of tightening, a sort of ache, a sort of clicking as stone was added to stone, as if someone were building a house inside her.

It was a Sunday morning and it was early and dark. The clock on the shelf read six. Rita lay in the warm dent of the mattress. There were a lot of things that she had to do but she didn't get up straight away. Through the wall, the woman next door shifted and laughed quietly in her sleep. The heating clicked on. She would need to turn that off, or set it for an hour in the middle of the day to stop the pipes freezing. It had been a cold winter. Most mornings there was ice inside the windows. Rita had an extra duvet and she had bought an electric blanket which could be switched on one half at a time so she didn't need to heat the empty side of the bed if she didn't want to. She liked practical things like that – she had a bottle of hand soap that could be used without water and jump-leads small enough to fit in a handbag.

A car drove past slowly. It had been snowing on and off for the past week. All along the street, snow was piled on cars and trees, all blues and purples and greys, and small icicles hung off the branches like the ghosts of leaves. Everything seemed quieter in the snow, quieter and further away, so that, lying there in bed, Rita had the vague feeling that if she got up and opened the curtains she would see that the world had packed up and moved on without her during the night. It was only a vague feeling though and she turned her thoughts to other things: jobs she needed to do, her plants, salt. When she was thinking like that, Rita often said words out loud, so that now she said 'lights', now she said 'teeth', but then she clenched her jaw because she didn't want to think about her teeth turning into stone; the awful, dry crumbliness of it.

She swung her legs out of bed and pulled thick socks over her feet. She went downstairs and into the kitchen. Before she did anything else, she got a glass of water and tipped salt into it and drank it down, crunching up the thick sediment at the bottom. She switched on the radio. 'Don't delay,' the end of an advert said. 'Visit Lighting World for all your lighting needs,' said another. She'd read somewhere that a man had bought a lamp from there and it had caught fire. The smell of burnt plastic followed him for days. The news came on. 'More snow is expected. Temperatures reaching down to minus ten in places.' Rita filled up the kettle and put it on. There was a cold breeze from nowhere and suddenly she was up on the cliffs with the other standing stones, watching a buzzard rising and circling on its huge spread of wings. Then she was back in front of the kettle again and it had boiled.

She drank her tea and made toast, which she ate cold and dry. She rinsed the plate, never wanting to wash up outside of work; crumbs floating around in water could put her off food for days. Afterwards she checked the fridge to see if there was anything in there that would go off if she was away a long time. There wasn't much: a portion of lasagne she'd been planning to have that night, a block of cheese, half a yellowing onion, milk. She didn't know how long she would be away. There were people from the town who had been standing up in the circle for years – five, twelve, thirty. Rita had changed three times before and each time it had lasted less than a month. But you could never be sure. There was always the possibility that next time it would be for much longer. After a while, somebody would let themselves in and turn off your heating, your boiler. They would tidy things up and sort out the post on the doormat. They would turn off your fridge.

She went back upstairs and stood in her bedroom. It was small and dark. On one shelf there was a row of porcelain animals – deer and horses and owls – that she had kept from when she was a child. There was also a small trophy which wasn't engraved and she couldn't remember what she had won it for, or if she had even won it at all.

She made the bed. She picked up her hairbrush and sat on the edge of the bed and started to brush her hair. She thought it had become paler: she was thirty-six and she thought that over the last few years it had become paler. She could never shift the stale bread and onion smell that working at the café left in it. Once in a while, if she looked at a magazine in a waiting room or saw an advert on TV, she would think about dying it, but she never did. She brushed her hair and tried not to think about it changing to stone, how heavy it would get, how it would drag on her neck and then clog up like it was full of grit, knitting together and drying and splitting and matting. She brushed and brushed her hair.

She was watering the plants and moving them into the warmest places in the house when the phone rang.

'Hi Rita,' Danny said. 'You enjoying the snow?' He always sounded nervous on the phone – Rita could tell that he was drawing stars all over the notebook he kept on the living-room table. He had pages and pages of stars.

'It was nice the first day,' she said. 'Now I want it to stop.'

'Yeah, me too. Now everyone just wants it to stop. Except the kids, of course. No kid ever wants it to stop. It wreaks havoc, doesn't it? Snow wreaks havoc.'

'It can do.' She waited for him to say what he was ringing for. Probably the snow had stopped something of his working. They had broken up five years ago but before that they had been together for eight. They still stayed in touch and saw each other now and again. Eight years was a long time; too long just to stop seeing somebody completely. It didn't seem right to stop seeing somebody completely. They still went out for dinner together on their birthdays. Sometimes Danny would stay over, and in the morning they would take it in turns to shower. Danny always took too long and Rita would sit on the bed listening to him using up all the hot water and singing the long, strange ballads he always sang.

'It can wreak havoc with a lot of things, can't it?' Danny said again. 'Cars, for one thing. How many cars do you know that work perfectly when it snows?'

'Mine works OK,' she told him.

'I just think that as soon as it snows, bam, most cars just give up.'

Rita let a moment pass. 'Your car won't start.'

'Not really,' he admitted. 'I'd take it into a garage, but it's a Sunday.'

'Don't you have breakdown cover?' she asked, already knowing he would have forgotten to renew it. 'Do you need it today?'

'Yeah,' he said. 'It just gave up. But listen Rita, don't worry about it. I'm sure I can sort something out.'

She looked around the kitchen. Maybe she could spare an hour. An hour wasn't such a long time and it was only half past ten.

'I'll take a quick look,' she told him.

Her own car started up fine. She poured hot water over the windscreen and then scraped the rest of the ice off. As she got in, icy feathers started to grow back over the glass. She drove slowly past the banked-up snow. Town was mostly empty – a few shops and cafés open on winter hours, a walker looking at the derelict cinema. There were snowmen everywhere, most of them with arms or eyes slipping off and their bodies tipping over. She passed a snowman wearing glasses, its head tilted back so that it was staring up at the sky.

As she got closer to Danny's, she saw that the weathervane that always pointed the same way had been taken down and a house had been painted yellow. Danny still lived in the flat they had rented together. They had lived there a long time and sometimes she missed this part of town. Afterwards, Rita had rented a one-bedroom house, and when the landlord put it up for sale a few years later she bought it. It wasn't the house she had expected to buy, it was cold and small and didn't let in much light, but it was what had come up.

She drove slowly down her old street, waved to someone she used to know. She pulled into the road outside the flat and parked. The snow in the road was packed down hard. A cold wind blew in off the sea. Her feet felt heavy and cold and her ankles were stiff. Stone grated inside her boots. The front steps were icy and she went up them carefully and rang the bell. Danny opened the door and smiled. He was tall and had to stoop in doorways. 'I've just got to find my coat,' he said.

She went into the hall to wait. It always smelled musty and garlicky. There was the broken tennis racket that had been there when they moved in, and the junk mail piled up next to the shoes and coats. Danny had recently been made a partner in the advertising company he worked at and now there were shiny black shoes, the kind he hated, among all the trainers.

'I'm still getting post for Miriam Burns,' he said. He pointed to a pile of cellophane-wrapped magazines on the floor. 'I get at least two every month.' When they had lived together, almost all their post had been for other people: repossession warnings, final bills. 'Return to sender,' Rita had written on everything.

Danny put his coat on over a faded T-shirt. Rita recognised almost all of his clothes, but they were starting to look slightly too small on him. He should get some more but he hated getting rid of anything, used to stop her throwing away flowers until the stems were bare.

'I can't stay long,' she said.

They went out to Danny's car. He got in and tried the engine. It didn't make any noise, not even a splutter. He kept trying but nothing happened. Rita tried the ignition herself then went round and opened the bonnet. Everything in there was cold and icy. There was ice around the dipstick when she checked the oil. Jump-leads wouldn't start it. She shook her head. 'It's not going to start,' she said. 'You'll have to wait until tomorrow and get towed.'

Danny tried the engine once more. 'I have to be somewhere this afternoon.'

'Can't you put it off?'

He stayed sitting in the driver's seat with the door open. Rita watched the shape of each breath appear as it hit the cold air. Finally he got out of the car and slammed the door and she followed him up the steps to the flat.

He went through the hall and into the living room. Their old sofa was there – she'd let him keep it – and the one blue wall that Danny had started painting then given up. She had a sudden memory of Danny painting blue on her cheek and then kissing her up against the wall but she pushed it out of her mind. 'I knead you,' he used to say, rubbing her shoulders, her stomach. She pushed it out of her mind. She had to get going; she had a lot of things to do. She made a list in her head: lock the windows, phone work, move the plants. Or had she already moved them?

'I had a viewing,' Danny said. 'For a house. I can't make it in the week.' He kept his coat on. He rearranged a pile of newspapers on the table. There were the pages of stars.

'You're moving?'

'Apparently it's got loads of space. I need a bigger place. I've got this new job now and I should move somewhere bigger.' He stacked and restacked the newspapers. 'It's a good deal, better than anything I could get in town. I mean, Jesus, I've been renting this place for ever.'

Rita listened, knowing already that she would take him to see the house, knowing that Danny knew she would.

It was only twenty minutes away. It would be an hour and a half round trip maximum, Rita thought as she and Danny got into her car. An hour and a half max and then she would go home and sort everything out. She'd be back by lunchtime. She needed to be back by lunchtime. The bottoms of her legs had started to feel cold, as if she were standing in the sea. Soon the cold would rise up until it felt like she was wading knee-deep, waist-deep, shoulder-deep in water.

'Apparently it's a good deal,' Danny said again as Rita started the car. 'Better than anything I could get in town.' He turned the radio on and when there was nothing playing that he wanted, he rummaged around in the glove box and found a couple of the old mix tapes he used to make. He liked to listen to Chopin next to the Eagles. He put one on and leaned back.

Houses and fields went by.

'You need to take the next left,' Danny said after a while.

They drove slowly for another mile but no left turn came up. They passed a house with washing out on the line, all the sheets frozen stiff and leaning out at angles like roofs.

'We've missed it,' Danny said after a while. 'We've missed the turn.' He looked round and back at the road. 'There should have been a left turn.'

'I didn't see a left turn,' Rita said. She pulled in and turned round. There were tyre marks all over the snow and it was easy to see the places where others cars had skidded. All around, the fields were covered in snow and the trees were edged with snow, so that the trees almost disappeared into the sky.

They drove back the way they had come. After a while, Danny

pointed out a turning and they took it. It led on to a single-track road. It hadn't been gritted and the wheels spun on ice. Rita changed down to first gear. She really didn't want to get stuck out there. So far they had been driving almost an hour.

There was a cluster of stone houses and a church and they parked at the side of the road. The church bells chimed the half-hour. They got out of the car. Snow slid off a tree and on to the pavement.

'The estate agent said the neighbour would let me in,' Danny said. He checked that Rita's door was locked; she'd only forgotten once but now he checked every time.

'Which neighbour?'

'It's that house,' he said, pointing. They walked towards it and waited at the front, clapping their hands together and breathing on them. A dog barked over and over. Danny paced around then walked down the street, looking at the other houses. 'I'm pretty sure it's this one,' he said, coming back. He always started off certain, then slipped quickly into uncertainty. He hadn't brought the address. They went through the front garden. There were frozen pieces of bread mixed in with the snow.

A man came out of the house next door holding a key. He was wearing a dressing-gown and slippers shaped like wine bottles.

'Are you two here for the viewing?' he asked. 'I'm surprised you made it in this. I wasn't expecting you.' He handed Rita the key. 'I didn't know her very well myself,' he said, nodding at the house. 'I did ask if she needed anything once and she told me she didn't. Maybe I should have taken round some milk, or the paper, but she said she didn't need anything.' He looked at them as if he wanted some kind of answer, his eyes blurry as old glass.

'Thanks,' Danny said. 'We'll drop them back.' Rita gave him the key and he unlocked the door and let them in.

The house was freezing. At first glance it looked completely empty but there was a doormat at the entrance and an umbrella leaning against the wall.

Danny hesitated by the door. 'Do you think she died in the house?' he asked.

'Why would that matter?' Rita said. She walked past him and went through the hall and into the living room. She wondered if they should have taken their shoes off but didn't go back. All the time she was thinking: lock the windows, phone work, move the plants.

The living room was big and cold. The windows looked out over the churchyard. All the gravestones faced the same way. There was a boarded-up fireplace and a wooden chair in one corner of the room. They walked round it once, looking at the skirting, the ceiling. The floorboards creaked. The ceilings were high and there was a light socket but no bulb. As she was walking round, Rita thought about the position of the room, how much it would take to heat, but then she stopped herself; it wasn't her house, she didn't need to think about those things. She couldn't imagine Danny sitting in this big room, though, with cold light streaming through. Their old sofa. She stopped herself thinking about it. She leaned against the stone wall. She felt the stone in her legs reaching out towards the wall so that for a second she couldn't tell where it stopped and her legs began. She moved away. She watched Danny. He ran his hands around the window frame. Bits of the wood were flaking off.

'Do you think these would be draughty?' he asked. 'They feel draughty.'

Old windows like that were always draughty. 'Maybe a bit,' she told him.

'Only a bit, though, right?' Danny said.

Just as they were going out through the door, they heard a scuffling, scratching noise coming from behind them. Rita went back into the room. There wasn't anything there and the noise stopped almost as quickly as it had begun. It was probably just snow falling off the roof.

Danny was already back in the hall. 'There are three bedrooms,' he said. 'It's a good deal for three. Shall we look at them first, or the kitchen?' He had his hands jammed in his coat pockets and his shoulders hunched up.

'Three bedrooms?' Rita asked. Then after a pause she said, 'The kitchen.' The kitchen was an important room. It was where children would be, if there were children. She wondered if there would be any salt left behind in a cupboard.

'You could put a huge table in here,' Danny said as soon as they went in. 'One of those huge ones with about ten chairs.' He stood back as if he were already looking at it.

'So you could make cheesy beans for everyone?' Rita said. She laughed but Danny didn't laugh. He could probably make more things now. The house was quiet. Outside, someone called out. A bird landed on the window-sill, scrabbled around, then flew off again.

Danny was looking out of the window and on to the back garden, which was covered in a thick layer of snow. There was a stone wall around it. The snow was smooth with no footprints. A picnic table was up to its ankles. As they looked out, a few small flakes fell slowly, lightly, like spiders.

'It might start snowing harder soon,' Rita said.

They went upstairs. Rita's feet were getting heavier and harder to lift. It took her longer than it should to go up the stairs. Halfway, she heard the scratching noise again and she paused for a second to listen. It didn't sound like snow that time.

Danny was looking at the bathroom. Rita glanced round the door, thinking about the snow. There was a towel that had been left behind next to the sink. It was exactly the same one that she had, blue with white stripes. For a second, she thought it was hers.

'The tiles in there remind me of something,' Danny said, coming out. He took a few steps down the hall and then went back and looked in again. 'The colour.'

Rita paced outside the bathroom. 'It might snow harder soon,' she said.

'It's not meant to,' Danny said. 'I heard it was going to stop.'

In the first bedroom, there was a pair of slippers under the bed. Danny looked around the room, but his eyes kept shifting towards the slippers. There was a hush to the house which was more than the hush of an empty house – it was the hush of somewhere almost empty. There was a sweet smell in the air, as if someone had just moved through it wearing perfume, or someone had just taken away a vase of flowers. It felt like, at any moment, they would meet someone coming round a corner or see a hand opening a door.

'You like built-in wardrobes,' Danny said. 'They're practical, right?'

Rita was over by the door but she came back to look. 'That one smells of camphor.'

'Camphor? How do you know what camphor smells like? No one knows what camphor smells like.' He leaned right in, half expecting heavy fur coats, the smell of snow in the distance, such a strong image he often mistook it for his own memory.

'It smells like camphor,' Rita said, knowing that part of him was pushing through fur coats. She circled the joints of her knees, trying to keep them moving. They were aching and stiff. She had to concentrate hard on where she was, because more and more often she found herself back up at the cliffs with the other standing stones, watching the buzzard, watching the clouds fill up with snow. Her knees felt like they had a blood-pressure band around them, slowly getting tighter and tighter.

'This wardrobe is probably about as big as our old bathroom.' He closed it.

'Bigger, probably,' Rita said. It was so cold in the house. She pulled her coat tighter.

'There's a leak in it somewhere.'

'Wardrobes don't leak.'

'In the old bathroom,' Danny said. 'In the corner.'

She remembered fixing a leak in the old bathroom. She had plastered over the crack but the plaster had probably weakened by now. She would have to show Danny what to do about it, or maybe just tell him to ring the landlord.

'You should look at the other rooms,' she said. She waited out in the hall. After a while, she heard the scratching sound start up again downstairs, louder this time. It sounded like something shuffling backwards and forwards across a room.

She went downstairs and into the living room. She waited a while. The noise was coming from the fireplace. She knelt down and tried to move the board. It was wedged in tightly. She heard Danny come down the stairs and into the room. 'I need you to help me move this.'

'What are you doing?' he asked.

'Moving the board.'

He came over and leaned down and hooked his fingers over the top. Rita dug a finger into a gap in the side and they pulled. The board came loose and swung open, grating against the stone.

The fireplace was dark. They stared in. It was dark but they could see something moving. There was a scuffling noise and something burst out of it, skimming their faces.

'Jesus Christ!' Danny yelled, and they both jerked back. The bird flew in circles close to the ceiling. It looked like a sparrow but it was hard to tell because it was covered in soot. It started bumping against the ceiling, sending down small showers of soot on to the carpet. Danny backed away from it. The bird was panicking and it made the room seem smaller and closer. Its wings brushed against the plaster.

Rita walked slowly around the edge of the room and opened the window as wide as it would go. Cold air and a few flakes of snow came in. It was snowing harder now. There were soot marks on the ceiling and wall. Rita tried to usher the bird out. It flew towards the window then landed on the curtain rail. She moved the chair so it was under the rail and then reached for the bird. She leaned against Danny's shoulder. Just as she was getting close, the bird flew out the door and into the hall.

Danny ran out and opened the front door. Rita got down slowly from the chair. It was difficult; she was off balance. It was hard to bend each leg without her knees locking. She could feel the pull of the cliffs, could see them deep-ridged and braced against the wind.

'It went out,' Danny said. There was a single snowflake melting in his hair.

'We don't want to get stuck here,' Rita said.

As they slid the board back over the fireplace, she knocked her hip against the stone and it made a hollow clack. Danny stood in the middle of the room, looking round once more. The snowflake had melted and disappeared.

'Come on,' she said.

He closed the door and locked it.

'I'll keep my fingers crossed for you,' the neighbour said when Danny gave him the keys.

The engine didn't turn over all the way the first time Rita tried. Her heart gave a heavy thump. It started the second time. They drove back down the narrow lane. The tyre marks they had made on their way had almost been cancelled out by the snow. They were quiet in the car. Rita was concentrating on the road and on using the pedals with her stiff legs. Snowflakes landed and piled up on the windscreen.

The road they needed to turn on to was closed. There was a police sign across the middle. The yellow diversion signs pointed left.

'Shit,' Rita said.

'Maybe there was an accident,' Danny said. 'There must have been an accident if it's a police sign.'

Rita turned left. She couldn't envisage where the diversion would take them, or how long it would add to the journey back. There weren't any other cars on the road. Everywhere was quiet and empty. Danny didn't turn the music back on. The heater whirred out warm air. Rita tapped her hand against the steering-wheel and hunched forwards. She drove slowly with her lights on, tried not to think about the car stranded at the side of the road, a painful walk in God knows what direction.

She followed two more diversion signs before they were back on the main road and she knew where they were.

'Do you know what Jack said to me the other day?' Danny said. He leaned back in his seat. 'He said that he and Sally are going to get a cat.'

'What kind of cat?' Rita hadn't seen Jack and Sally for a long time. They were more Danny's friends.

'I don't know. One of those rescue ones, I think.'

'I can't imagine them with a cat.'

'That's what I thought,' Danny said. 'That's exactly what I

thought.' He stretched his legs out. He seemed to take up the whole car. 'I thought that rescue cats could have real problems anyway, that you could wake up and find all your clothes ripped up, or dead rabbits under your bed or something.'

She drove slowly past banked-up snow. A few more flakes hit the windscreen. Danny started talking about work and his longer hours. Rita could tell he was tired because his right eye got slightly lazy, the iris edging outwards like an orbiting planet. Sometimes, when he was really tired, he saw things: a hand waving in front of him, hundreds of horses at the side of the road. It used to scare her, when they were driving back from somewhere at night and he would say, 'Look at all the horses,' and there would be nothing but an empty road. Now she found herself watching him, slipping back into watching him, and she had to stop herself; she made herself concentrate on driving, on moving her stiff legs. Her stomach was hardening from the inside outwards, in rings like an old tree growing and hardening.

'Hey, remember that cat you found and wanted us to keep?' Danny asked. 'You made it a bed in a box and fed it bits of potato.' He laughed. 'I told you we had to find the owners.'

'You hit it with your car,' Rita said. 'We had to look after it until we found the owner.'

Danny stopped laughing. He frowned. 'No I didn't.'

'You did,' Rita said. 'It was OK, though, you didn't hit it hard.'

'That cat was just lost.' He wiped at his fogged-up window. Snow had gathered on the pane. He frowned again and wiped the window.

Rita wiped her own window with her glove, ended up smearing it more. 'You're right,' she said at last. 'I think it probably was just lost.'

The road turned into a wide, residential street. They were almost back. She needed more salt. When they pulled in outside Danny's flat, it was almost three o' clock. She was desperate for more salt. She went inside with Danny and while he was taking off his shoes and coat, she went into the kitchen and poured herself a glass of water and tipped salt into it. Her hands were stiff and cracked. She fumbled with the glass and the tap. Danny came in just as she was finishing it, saw the salt pot out on the table. 'Rita,' he said. She shook her head. He looked at her feet, imagining the stone inside her boots.

He walked her to the door. He was tall; he had to stoop in doorways.

Her own house was cold. She kept her coat and scarf on. Already, as it always did when this happened, the house felt not quite her own: the furniture, the wallpaper, the small noises. She didn't have long. She didn't have time to phone work or to lock all the windows. She took out the bin bag but she couldn't tie it up so she just folded the top over as well as she could. She clenched and unclenched her hands, trying to loosen them. Bending down was becoming difficult because of her hips and back. Her whole body was aching and tightening. As she bent, she could feel the discs in her back grating over one another, like an old gate opening over stones.

Rita locked the door, left the key under the mat and went back outside. It was snowing harder now and flakes fell in fat patches on her shoulders and in her hair. She walked down the road and past all the houses. It wasn't a long walk. She was glad it wasn't long. Soon, the houses turned to fields and then cliffs and she walked up along the cliff path. The cliffs were covered in a light, ridged coating of snow. It hadn't settled as thickly on them as it had in town. The sea was light grey and still and the sky was light grey and still and it was hard to tell one from the other.

It was a struggle to walk now. It was difficult to breathe. Her legs grated together and her hips didn't rotate. Her back was locked and rigid. She had her hands in her pockets and she clenched them and then couldn't unclench them again. They stayed in tight fists in her pockets.

The standing stones loomed out ahead through the snow. They made up a large, rough circle, set back from the edge of the cliff in a patch of long grass. Some were tall, some short, some leaning outwards, one had fallen over completely. There were fifteen stones there, but the number changed all the time. Some of them looked new, others were covered in lichen, which was white and webbed and looked as if the snow were creeping up the stone. There was an extra quietness that hovered around the circle, especially today, surrounded by the weather. Rita could imagine how cold each stone would feel if she touched them.

She felt exhausted. She dragged herself down the path and reached the stones. She stood in a gap and waited. Snow was falling lightly and whirling in the wind up on the cliffs. The wind pushed the flakes in one direction like lines of static. Over the sea, the water and the snow and sky were one grey haze. The wind keened faintly and when Rita looked up she saw a buzzard, circling and rising above her.

She could feel the little clicks of stone against stone as her shoulders seized up and turned rigid. She made sure she was facing out to sea. The stone moved up into her neck and soon she couldn't turn it at all. She chose a spot on the horizon to look at and after a while she couldn't look away. She wasn't afraid. The first time she had been afraid but she wasn't any more. Breathing stopped, but there was a different kind of breathing. She let her thoughts wander.

She thought of Danny, and of the house they had been to see. Did she like the house? She felt confused when she thought of it. Was she meant to have liked the house or not? The snow blurred it all so she couldn't even remember where the house was. It was a relief, really. The whole thing was a relief. There was the house somewhere in the snow; there was the snow in Danny's hair. She let her thoughts wander and they swooped upwards like birds, so that now she thought of a bird flying round a room, now she thought of someone singing, of marbles, of someone laughing in their sleep, of a bird flying round a room, of one lovely eye moving, of the wind, of lichen, a buzzard circling, a single snowflake, thrift, lichen and the wind.

# Of Mothers and Little People

YOU ARRIVE EARLY and move quietly through your childhood house. You haven't been here for months, or maybe over a year, and many things catch your eye: the lovely, smooth dents inside the washing machine that you used to run your palms over; the lopsided clock you made at school; vases with nothing but water inside. Why does your mother always have empty vases around? You've never asked. The late birthday card you sent is behind a banana magnet on the fridge. You open it. Your handwriting is terrible – rushed and sprawling over the shiny paper like dropped stitches. *Sorry I couldn't make it in the end, you know what it's like, work, work, work, meetings . . .* There is always work and there are always meetings.

You drop your bag down on the carpet and go upstairs to find your mother. You want to surprise her. She will probably be busy preparing for your visit: maybe putting a book you might like on your bedside table, maybe dusting the bedside table with small, quick strokes. This is how you always think of her: watering plants in front of the dark kitchen window, or slowly scraping ice out of the freezer, small flakes melting around her knees; or just sitting, early in the morning, next to the radiator and her collection of decorated eggs. You imagine that she collects these eggs because she is, first and foremost, a mother. You tell Barnaby, the friend at work you are sleeping with, that you worry about your mother and those bright, patterned eggs. 'Eggs?' Barnaby says. 'Mine's allergic to eggs. Her throat swells up like a balloon. She has to carry a shot around in a necklace.' He watches his screensaver as it flings out millions of tiny stars. But what you don't know is that, long before your father left, he bought your mother the first egg randomly and impulsively, and after that, for birthdays and Christmases, everybody else followed suit, foisting eggs upon her like extra helpings of dessert.

As you reach the landing, you hear her in the bathroom. She is talking to herself. She has done this as far back as you can remember – you hardly even notice it any more. You are thinking of the best way to announce yourself, something exuberant and witty, something to really make her day. What you want to do is banish all those lonely, quiet moments that you imagine are like cobwebs nestling in every corner of the house. What would be the best way? When you were six, you used to forward-roll through doorways and clatter heavily into her legs, or you would creep forwards across the shiny kitchen lino and wrap yourself around her feet. Sometimes, she would start walking over to the dishwasher, dragging you along slowly behind her like a mop, pretending that she didn't notice you were there.

You move forwards until you can see through the open bathroom door. There is your mother, leaning over the sink. She is wearing her gardening clothes – the baggy jeans with the damp brown knees and the red checked shirt that feels rough and scratchy against your cheek. Looking at your mother, you see her in smells and in touch, but really, you haven't touched her properly for years. You are always rushing as you leave, hugging her loosely and briefly, so that, later on in the car, you only have a faint impression of her small body against yours.

Now you are standing right in the doorway but she hasn't seen you. She has taken a small blue pot from inside the cupboard and is unscrewing the lid. She is absorbed – you don't think she would notice you if you coughed. You have seen this pot before. It was always kept on the highest shelf along with her razor and her prescriptions. You watch as she scoops out some thick cream and rubs it slowly over her eyelids. The cream leaves a strange, bluish shimmer over them, like the shimmer of fish scales or oil rainbowing a puddle. She rubs until all the cream has vanished, wincing as she does it. When she opens her eyes, you imagine for a second that the whites have been stained a pale green, but almost immediately they are white again. She blinks into the mirror and when she finally turns round and sees you, she doesn't even jump. 'Here you are,' she says. You nod to confirm it, suddenly feeling big and invasive in her bathroom doorway. When she places her hand on the small of your back to guide you downstairs, towards the kettle, towards your favourite biscuits, you feel your own loneliness banished, you feel saved, which you don't think is exactly the right way around. It isn't exactly as you planned it. But in any case, you have arrived.

It is still warm enough to sit in the garden. You tip up the plastic chairs to drain the water off the seats and flick off the maple leaves. The garden is small and yellow and brown and red. It drips with leftovers from the last shower of rain. The smell of wet soil in this garden is as familiar to you as the smell of your own hair. You can smell the sea here too, spreading its salty hands through the air. You tell your mother how strange it is to be somewhere so quiet. In your

41

flat in the city, cars and trains bellow past without cease. You don't have a garden, but once or twice, you and Barnaby have crawled out of the window on to next door's roof and lain there like children gaping up at the sky.

Your mother asks about your job. She is always interested in it. She works part-time in a bakery and has never used a computer. She thinks that the internet is a dangerous device for social control. You told that to your boss, Rachel. 'Sweet,' she said. 'That's really sweet. She reminds me of my mother. She doesn't think you can microwave cling film, isn't that crazy?'

You tell her about the project you have just finished working on. You had to compile a report about customer satisfaction for a range of hotels. Many of the customers did not enjoy their stay. Some got locked in their rooms and had to bang on the door for help. Others found someone else's crisps or socks or clumps of hair. They did not like the view out of the window or the self-service breakfast. 'Your toaster does not toast!' they wrote on the questionnaires. 'I had to put the slice through four times!' Every year, you make action plans for the hotel chain. In the action plan last year you suggested new toasters. This year, you suggested new toasters. It is in these small moments that you doubt the value of your work. This is a secret fear and one that you do not tell your mother. Perhaps you almost have, once or twice, but she has seemed distracted at those moments, shifting on her seat, rubbing her shoulder or the back of her neck. Anyway, you are generous, you do not want to burden her with your worries and leave her with them once you have driven away.

'Work is A-OK,' you say (you only ever say 'A-OK' around your mother. You also say 'okey-dokey' a lot and 'Brillopads!'). 'I got a new chair and a phone that says good morning to me when I come in.'

'The chair says good morning?' she asks.

'Only the phone says that,' you say. 'The chair is just a normal chair.' She shakes her head, amazed at a talking phone or disappointed in the chair, you can't really tell. 'Although, when the chair swivels it squeaks and sounds as if it's talking sometimes, and, get this, Barnaby makes up this mouse voice and he . . .' You trail off, realising that your mother wouldn't get the joke. The trees bend and shiver; they sound as though they are rifling through their own leaves for something lost.

You're about to tell your mother this but then a neighbour whose name you have forgotten walks past the fence and leans over. He smiles at your mother and laughs a lot. He has thick white hair and one of those ruddy glows which mean he is either outdoorsy or drunk. You wonder whether he will ask her out. Maybe he already has, although as far as you are aware, she has not been with anybody since your father left nine years ago. Now your father is getting married to a woman called Rhea he met at the aquarium. Rhea works at the aquarium, your father explained when he phoned you about it. She has a thing about fish. 'What about my mother?' you shouted at him, about seven years too late.

'Myopia?' he asked. The phone line buzzed with static – it's a bad connection, you always mishear each other on it, your conversations full of gaps and holes that you spend hours trying to fill in later.

You were worried about how to tell your mother, but when you finally did, she invited them over for a celebration lunch. This is why you are back this weekend. The lunch is tomorrow and, thankfully, you are between projects. You assume that she needs moral support – the invitation must be some kind of complicated, masochistic act. He left her! She shouldn't cook for him; she should at least buy in some kind of ready meal. You are ready to fight some kind of battle.

'You should get a date for this lunch,' you tell her once the neighbour has left. Your mother says something inaudible and starts to clear the table. The cold and damp in the air have turned the high points in her cheeks and the tip of her nose a dark pink. To you, your mother is still the most beautiful person who ever lived. You don't say this. Instead you say, 'If you squint, that man could almost definitely be attractive. Almost like Steve Martin.' *Roxanne* is her favourite film. She swats at you with a tea-towel. When you're back inside, you show her the ready-made Yorkshire puddings you have brought along to help out.

You cook dinner together – something with spaghetti and cream and lots of garlic bread. 'Customers say their dinners are sixty-eight per cent more enjoyable if they include garlic bread,' you tell your mother. There is a film on TV that you both want to watch so you curl your legs up underneath you and share a blanket on the sofa. Your toes are almost touching. The film is not as good as you remembered. The happy ending is forecast from the very first scene. You drift off but your mother gets caught up in it and tries not to cry at the end. You remembered it being more realistic. There should be more films where couples drift apart slowly and without properly noticing until it's too late, when they say things to each other like, 'Which one of us bought that extension lead? No seriously, did you buy that extension lead or did I, because we're both going to need that.'

The film makes you feel morose and lonely, but then you remember you've got Barnaby. You haven't told your mother about him yet. You're not sure how to talk about your relationship; whenever you think about it you feel confused and bored, as if you were trying to do a cryptic crossword. Either talk to her about Barnaby now or don't. If you do, she will ask what he is like. Think for a while. Say he has the softest back you have ever felt; say he likes to answer his mobile as if his answerphone has picked up, so that you start to leave a message then realise it's been him all along. Tell her how he really, really likes to do that.

'Home?' Barnaby said when you told him your weekend plans. You were lying in bed, his lips grazing your ear. 'Going home?' he said again. 'What do you call this place then?' And you just shrugged, suddenly unsure, feeling yourself in-between: the empty corridors of it, the neither-here-nor-there of it.

Once your mother has gone to bed, you prowl around the house. You have a few glasses of various drinks you find in the cupboard. You used to sit under the kitchen table for hours as a child, so you get in there and sit cross-legged with your head bowed down. It isn't as relaxing as you remember so you unfold, crawl out and go upstairs to the bathroom. Your mother's dressing-gown is on the back of the door and you put it on. The sleeves are too short for you. It is an old dressing-gown and it smells of that smell your mother has which you cannot place – some flowers you don't recognise, or a perfume that she doesn't seem to actually wear. Her things are scattered all around the bathroom and you look through them. There are shampoos and soaps and creams. This is your mother, here, in products. You rub her hand cream into your hands and you brush your teeth with her toothpaste. At one point, you take out that blue pot of cream and open the lid. You smell it, but it doesn't smell of anything. You scoop some out and rub it over your eyes, hoping for the lovely blue shimmer it left on her lids. When you open them, there is a sudden sharp pain. Your eyes stream. Your eyelashes seem to be tightening. In a panic, you splash water all over your face and after a while the stinging goes away and you can open your eyes. They seem to turn pale green for a second, and then white again. You must be allergic to the ingredients; maybe there is orange extract in there, or walnuts. You look for the label but there isn't one.

You decide to go to bed. In the hallway, you pass one of her empty vases, except that it isn't empty any more. The whole vase is bursting with bright leaves. You must have drunk more than you thought. Drinking has never agreed with you, and you keep telling yourself this when you check the other vases and see that they too are filled with leaves and flowers and that there is now ivy curling over the banister.

The sheets on your single bed are your old favourites: Aladdin and Jasmine kneeling on a magic carpet. Their faces are faded and grey, the colours all washed out. You get underneath the covers and ring Barnaby on your mobile. The green light makes it look like you're in an underwater cave. His phone rings and the answer-phone beeps in. Wait for the beep and say hello and wait for him to reply. 'Hello?' you say. 'Hellooo?' But it's his actual answerphone this time and your message will sound like you are lost, and somewhere very far away.

In the morning, you resolve to tell your mother to throw out that face cream. It has probably gone off – your mother never throws anything away. Rifling through the medicine box early on to get some paracetamol, you find cough linctus that is seven years past its use-by date and an old, dry packet of foot powder with a price label that is pre-decimal. You go back upstairs and sit in bed, waiting for her to get up. You have never liked houses early in the morning when no one else is around. They all have that still coldness that reminds you of museums, or the bright silence of empty swimming pools. She comes downstairs and pads into the kitchen. She switches on the kettle and you hear the clatter of cups and teaspoons, her quiet, early morning noises.

You pull on a jumper and go downstairs into the kitchen. You stop in the doorway. She is stirring tea with her back to you. There is a hand on her shoulder and it is not your hand. There is a man in the kitchen with his hand on your mother's shoulder. He is shorter than her and has dark, curly hair. He is wearing a waistcoat. His clothes are made from a strange material that sometimes looks green and sometimes looks silver.

You make some sort of sound and they both turn around to look at you. Your mother smiles her normal smile and asks if you would like tea. She asks how you slept. She is making two cups, not three: one for her and one for you. You wait for her to say something. You wait for him to say something. She doesn't say anything. He doesn't say anything. The man isn't even looking at you any more. You fiddle with your sleeves, your ears; you tie and re-tie your pyjama ribbon. Your mother hands you a cup of tea. You drink a big gulp straight away and burn the inside of your mouth and your lips. Your mother is acting as if the man isn't there so she obviously can't see him, and so you are obviously going mad, or something has damaged part of your brain. You have only taken drugs once, in fear of this, and so for it to have happened anyway seems a waste – you might as well have taken more. The man stays close to your mother as she tells you all about the lunch she is going to cook. Without pausing, she puts her arm behind her back and the man in the green waistcoat holds it. She does this so smoothly, so naturally, that you realise it is something she has been doing for a long time.

You are not sure if it takes seconds or minutes, but it suddenly strikes you that it is all to do with the cream. This man has always been there, right there, with your mother. He has appeared in front of your eyes like a slap in the face, like catching Santa outside the grotto reading *FHM*. You go upstairs and have a shower and get dressed. When you come back downstairs, your mother is standing at the oven cutting apples into a pan. The man in the green waistcoat is behind her with a hand on her hip. Her hip! You try not to stare. You try to act normally. You don't want them to know that you know.

You sit on the sofa and think. There was always that story you didn't really listen to, the one about your mother when she was younger, about her disappearing for months and then coming back like nothing had happened. The story hovered around your childhood but you never paid attention to it – after all, a lot of your friends' mothers had the same story to tell. You zoned out; there were always more important things. A couple of times, your friend Michelle tried to talk about it. 'My mum and yours were chosen to go there and look after all the little babies,' she told you.

'Where?' you asked her.

'I don't know. The woods, I think.'

'Why?'

'I don't know. They can't look after them by themselves. Someone has to do it for them. They're very small people. I don't think you can look after babies if you're that small.' Your mother never looked after any babies other than you! You glared at Michelle and poked her doll right in the eye.

Maybe, once or twice, your mother tried to talk to you about it. 'You know, when I was eighteen,' she would venture, over dinner, over breakfast. But you were always too busy, you never really listened; your own life was too important, too interesting, to hear about things that she used to do. All that was in the past, it was irrelevant, which was your favourite word at the time.

The doorbell rings. It is your father and Rhea. Oh God, you

had almost forgotten about your father and Rhea. The man in the green waistcoat squeezes your mother's shoulder in a supportive way. You get the door. This is the first time you have met Rhea. Straight away she touches your new short haircut and says you look like Betty Boop.

'More like David Hasselhoff,' you say.

She laughs loudly and repeats Betty Boop. She seems like a kind lady. Her own hair is the longest you have ever seen; she could probably sit on it. It is brown and a bit dry, with grey streaks behind her ears. When she hugs your mother, her tall, thin frame towers over her and her hair swings round each side, shutting them in together like a tent. Your mother and father kiss lightly on each cheek. Your father has put on some weight and he is wearing a baggy knitted jumper which is bright blue with orange fish on it. It turns out that Rhea knits, a lot. You will probably get something knitted for Christmas, your father whispers conspiratorially. The man in the green waistcoat leans against the kitchen cupboards and watches. He doesn't make any noise at all.

When everyone moves into the living room, on to sofas and chairs, he sits in the corner on the phone chair. It has a squishy leather pad but he doesn't make a dent in it. He moves when your mother moves, as if he is a green balloon that she has tied around her wrist. At one point he catches you looking at him and frowns, ever so slightly. He has a long, pointed nose and pale, high cheekbones. You carry on staring, trying to cross your eyes a little as if you are staring blankly into space, until he seems to relax. You watch your mother carefully. She is smiling and laughing. Sometimes she looks over at the man in the corner. If you didn't know that he was there you would think she was gazing wistfully into the distance.

Somehow, over lunch, the conversation gets on to your love life. You don't know how it happened: you were trying as hard as you could to avoid it. Rhea wants to know if you have a boyfriend. Your father wants to know how you can afford your flat if you are living in it alone. By now, the man in the green waistcoat is standing behind your mother's chair with his hands on her shoulders. He rubs her neck with his thumbs. Your mother rubs over his thumbs with her hands. This makes her look like she has a bad neck. You always thought she had a bad neck. You bought her a lavender-scented neck pillow last birthday which had to be heated up in the microwave. It smelled like yeast but she still used it.

'Neck still bad?' your father asks her.

'It's been better,' she says. You go and get the lavender neck pillow, heat it up for thirty seconds, and drape it over her neck, over the strange man's hands so that he has to move them. He sits back in the corner.

It strikes you that you are in a room of couples. It strikes you that they might all be feeling sorry for you. You can't decide whether you should be blasé about love, about relationships, or say that you and Barnaby are practically engaged. Opt for blasé. Say that you're seeing someone casually and with no strings. Say that you don't want to commit yourself. After all, you're young, you're a career woman. Seventy-two per cent of customers book a double room but occupy it singly. Rhea nods vigorously. She knows what you mean. She starts talking about the relationship habits of fish. Some of them are casual as hell, she says, especially the females. Female seahorses leave all the pregnancy stuff to the males. It seems like a much better arrangement. 'There's feminism for you,' she says. 'But then again, most female fish that give birth die a few months later but the males don't.' She shrugs and frowns.

'Nothing's perfect,' you say, pretending to know exactly what she is talking about. You ask if anyone wants coffee. Everyone does.

Afterwards, someone suggests a walk. It is a beautiful autumn afternoon. It is damp but sunny. The sky is clear. There are wet leaves everywhere. You walk along the road and then cut up a path that leads into the wood. The couples are holding hands. You are the odd one out: the fifth wheel, the kid who disturbs the babysitter and her boyfriend to ask for some milk. You wonder what would happen if you trod on the man in the green waistcoat's feet. Would you feel it? Would he feel it? He is right in front of you but you don't do it. Sometimes you think you can see the path through him. Your mother is talking to your father about lawnmowers because she needs a new one. He lists names and prices. He is a serious man who does a lot of research before he buys anything. He once had hiccups that lasted six months and now he rubs his throat a lot as he talks. You notice, underneath his thinning hair, that a few freckles have appeared, one by one, like murky stars.

A group of people walks towards you. They are dressed in water-proofs and have rucksacks and maps. You recognise the tall man in the middle with bright red hair: at fourteen, you thought he was the love of your life. You were convinced and planned a whole future together. As he walks closer, you catch his eye and then stick out your tongue, winking a big, cartoon wink. You used to do this to make him laugh. Your heart beats a little faster. You have always believed in fate, picturing it as a fairy godmother labouring over a huge timeta-ble. The man starts and squints and doesn't recognise you. He walks past. You've wasted a lot of time daydreaming about what would happen if you ever saw each other again. At least now you know. Your heartbeat slows down again.

The path enters the wood. It isn't a big wood, but once you're inside, it is hard to imagine where its edges are. As you walk, it increases ahead of you in roomfuls. The trees are in the last glorious stages of autumn colour. The ground is wet and there is moss everywhere, pushing up from the ground in thick cushions. The last of the wild garlic is dying back and so is all the bracken. It is an oak wood, but there are also elms and birches and holly trees, and all their branches are covered in lichen and ivy.

There is a faint path marked out by other people's feet. Here and there, you see scattered litter: cans, crisp packets; there is even a mattress leaning against a tree like an overgrown mushroom. Small orange mushrooms with frilled throats have colonised a tree stump. There are beech-nut husks all over the ground. Although you are still close to the road, you can't hear it in the wood. It is as if a door has swung shut behind you. You can hear a small stream somewhere and your own footsteps moving through earth and leaves. The wood smells damp and cold and of decay, but there is also a sweeter smell there – a half-familiar smell which you realise is the one that lingers around your mother's clothes.

The man in the green waistcoat is smiling. He has left the path and is wading through the dense, tangled parts of the wood. You can definitely see the trees through him now, and the material of his waistcoat is veined like a leaf. Your mother veers off the path towards him. She moves easily through the wood. There is a brown leaf curling into her hair. She disappears behind a trunk and you hear her laugh – or maybe it was a bird trilling, you are not sure.

A cuckoo cuckoos somewhere in the distance. A pigeon crashes through the tree next to you. There are two more pigeons scrabbling around on the ground. 'They're staring at us,' Rhea says. She has picked a handful of blackberries and is sharing them with your father, who never used to like them before.

You explain to them that pigeons are a hardy kind of bird. They eat what they can to survive. You respect this. Twelve per cent of customers won't eat the breakfast because it is not cooked to order. Pigeons don't expect cooked to order. If another animal threw up and there were seeds in it then they'd probably be happy.

It is cold and quiet. Your father has his arm around Rhea, a blackberry seed on his lip. Your mother appears and she blows a dandelion and the seeds rock weightlessly through the wood. She is standing next to you now and the man in the green waistcoat is holding her hand. You reach over and lift the leaf out of her hair. She turns and smiles at you. The light filtering through the canopy is green and gold and the shafts root themselves in the ground like so many trees.

You wonder when the cream will wear off. Will there be a point when you start to see the man in the green waistcoat fade like the reverse of a developing photo? When the ivy curling around the banisters hardens and turns back into wood and white paint? You watch your mother carefully. To everyone else, it looks like she is standing alone, wrapping her arms around herself. What you mistook for sadness is love.

You stare at her like this for a while then look away. When you look back his thumb is touching the smooth dip of her throat. Look again and they have gone – there are only the leaves rustling and the branches swaying in the wind. You can hear your mother's footsteps somewhere close by but you cannot see her. You hear her laugh, or maybe it was just a bird trilling, you are not entirely sure.

# Lights in Other People's Houses

*God keep us from rocks and shelving sands,*
*And save us from Breage and Germoe men's hands.*
Old sailors' prayer

THE MORNING THE WRECKER appeared was the hottest so far. The heat wave had been building slowly, gathering day by day. Tap water came out tepid. Paint split and peeled back; an empty glass that Maddy had left next to the window cracked.

Russell went from room to room, trying to find his shoes, his keys, his bike lock. He was running late again, always needing another ten minutes. 'Are you going to sort out a few of those boxes today?' he asked Maddy on his way through the kitchen.

Maddy was still in pyjamas and clutching her first mug of tea. She worked from home as an audio typist and it took her a while to get started. 'Your keys are here,' she said, pointing to the table. Russell had made the table himself. There was a knot in the wood that looked like a small, pale heart. Carpentry, Russell told her, is all about finding smaller shapes within bigger shapes – you have to be able to see what's inside, lurking.

'You should sort a few of them today,' he said. He leaned down to get his keys. 'You said you'd do them months ago.'

Maddy picked up the egg she'd hidden so she could pretend to pull it out of Russell's ear – a little trick she'd been practising. But he straightened up too quickly and she was left holding out the egg like an offering. 'I found an egg,' she said.

Russell looked at it for a second, frowning. The name badge pinned to his shirt was missing an 's'. Underneath it said 'Jem's Discount Hardware'. He kissed the top of her head, briefly, lightly. 'Remember the boxes, OK?' The door swung shut and locked behind him.

The kitchen clacked and hummed. Maddy switched on the radio. A song started playing then dissolved into static. She adjusted the frequency but the static got louder. It sounded like waves hissing and breaking. She missed living near water, missed the sea with a terrible ache, like hunger – she kept imagining that she could smell it in the house, this morning particularly, even though it was so far away. She turned the radio off.

The kitchen clacked and hummed. Russell's plants were wilting in their yoghurt pots. What type of seeds were they? Sweet peas? Cress? Maddy watered them but the water pooled on the dry soil and wouldn't sink in. She thought: out of yoghurt, great oaks will grow. Then, to the empty kitchen she said, 'Out of yoghurt, great oaks will grow.' She didn't know anyone in this town.

She picked up plates from the draining board and put them in the cupboard. She got a handful of spoons and forks and opened the cutlery drawer but there were receipts and bills crammed inside. They'd moved in together eight months ago and she was still opening the wrong drawers, sliding her hand up and down smooth walls to find a light switch. The flats above and below were empty. The landlord said he might sell the whole place soon. If he found a buyer he'd let them know, give them a month before they had to move out.

Maddy squatted down to open the bottom drawer and saw damp footprints on the floor.

They were boot prints, big and criss-crossed with sand. They hadn't been there before. They went across the kitchen, through the living room and into the hallway. The front door was still shut and locked. She stood up slowly and picked up the bread knife. She almost put it down again because there was something about holding a knife that made her feel more scared. A tip for an emergency started to go round and round in her head: 'If you are near water, get in and keep your head down.' What emergency was it for? Bees, probably. A swarm of bees.

There were noises coming from the spare bedroom. It sounded like ripping cardboard. There was low muttering. Maddy walked forwards quietly, hearing every footstep against the carpet. She stopped in the doorway and looked into the room. There was a pale, gaunt man sitting cross-legged on the floor, rifling through the boxes. His clothes and skin were wet and dripping. There was sand everywhere. His skin looked waxy, almost blue in places, and she knew immediately that he was a ghost by the strange restlessness he'd brought with him into the room, a restlessness and a clamouring, as if he had just disturbed a colony of nesting seabirds.

'What are you doing?' Maddy asked. She stayed by the door, lowered the knife.

'Sorting it,' the man said without looking up.

'That's my stuff.'

'It was left here.' He took out a vase and tested its weight. A faint, damp handprint bloomed on the glass then slowly evaporated.

'That's my stuff,' Maddy said again.

'I don't think so. It hasn't been touched for a long time.' It sounded like he was speaking from inside a cave – his voice was mournful and had a hollow echo. He had wide, bony shoulders and a matted beard covering wind-chapped skin. His eyes were faded, colourless. All the fingers on his left hand were curling inwards, as if he were clutching an invisible heart.

He was sorting everything into two piles. He put the vase on the biggest pile and then looked in another box. The vase was old and made of thick, green glass. Someone in Maddy's family had found it washed up on the beach. There was a smooth, raised pattern on it. Maddy couldn't remember what the pattern was, but she could feel her own five-year-old fingers running over it.

'That bit,' the man muttered. 'Those bits, not that.' He pulled the beads off an old pair of flip-flops, her mother's, the wicker soles cracked and spooling dust. He put the beads on one pile and the soles on the other. There was a photo album open on the floor next to him. There was Maddy's old house in sepia, run down even then, sprawling, all sagging roof and damp walls, eroded by the wind. There was her own face staring out of an upstairs window; there she was again, aged seven, climbing the magnolia that grew outside her bedroom, the flat grey sea in the distance.

The man sifted through the boxes slowly. He picked up a fragile teddy, shook his head and threw it on the smaller pile.

'What's wrong with that?' Maddy asked. The bear had been her grandmother's. It had two black buttons for eyes, a missing ear. 'There's nothing wrong with that.'

'Poor stitching,' the man said. 'You wouldn't get much for it.'

Maddy went over to the pile and picked the bear up. It was silky and musty. She breathed in its mothball smell. She had forgotten exactly what was in these boxes. When her parents had sold the house and moved away – for shops and people near by, they said, for dry air – they had packed light, deciding almost overnight to leave everything behind, start again.

'It's all become such a burden,' her mother confided, her voice suddenly wavering, old. 'It all piled up.' She shook her head, amazed at how it had happened. 'Get rid of it for us, Maddy, OK?' But instead, Maddy had dragged the boxes to the flat, promising Russell she'd sort it out over the next few days. She remembered the front door of the house shutting and locking for the last time behind her. She'd left her coat inside and only realised later.

'No good, no good,' the man said. There was an oil lamp next to him, big, with a brass handle.

'Who are you?' Maddy asked.

He got up, unfolding his legs stiffly. He was tall and stooping. He went over to the window and looked out and a layer of condensation appeared on the glass. 'It's hot,' he said. The smell of sea and beaches lingered around him: a rusty tin kind of smell, a whisky and rockpool smell, damp wood and salt and old seaweed.

Maddy watched drop after drop of water running down the window. Find water and keep your head down, she thought. 'Who are you?' she asked again.

'William Penna,' he said. 'Begat of Mary and Samuel Penna, begat of Nora and John Penna, begat of Simon and Selina Roberts, begat of Rachel and Hugh Roberts, begat of William and Theresa Draper.' He sighed. His front teeth were chipped and broken. 'Wreckers,' he said. He shook his head. 'I can't go back yet, I can't go back yet. Where am I?' he said. 'Where's all the water?' He craned his head out of the window. There were roofs then fields to the horizon.

'Maybe you could go back,' Maddy said. Go back, she thought. Go back.

'It's too hot. Getting hotter. The beach. People everywhere. More and more people. Music and food and people. All in the sea, all over the space, the cliffs,' the wrecker said. His face darkened and he carried on pacing. 'They shouldn't be there,' he said. 'There's not enough space.' He looked exhausted. He unfolded an old garden chair and sat down on it. Water sloshed over the tops of his boots. 'Where am I?' he asked again. Maddy thought she could hear waves rolling over and seagulls cawing inside his throat. He sat in the chair and stared out of the window.

Hours passed. The light began to fade. The wrecker didn't move. Eventually, Maddy came back in and packed up the boxes tight.

The wrecker lit his lamp and put it in the kitchen window. It was bright, but up close there was no warmth to the flame. You could put your whole hand in it. When the wrecker left the room, Maddy leaned over it and tried to blow it out, but the flame didn't even flicker.

Sand drifted on to carpets. The flat heated up. Russell's plants turned brown. The wrecker paced restlessly. The air around him was thick and humid and charged, as if he had just come indoors from walking in stormy weather. He watched daytime TV. He liked horse-racing and chat shows. He swapped the toothbrushes and the razors around in the bathroom. He sat among Maddy's boxes and looked through them, endlessly.

'Why is he here?' Russell whispered to Maddy. 'Why here?'

The TV flashed and blared. The wrecker looked at Russell from the other side of the room. 'Where am I?' he asked. 'Where's all the water?' He ran a bath and stood in it for hours. Salt dried to crystals in the corners of his eyes.

*　*　*

Nights stretched and grew longer. The wrecker had nightmares about drowning. Maddy lay awake listening to him thrashing, hacking up water, sending sand and stones thumping into the floor.

'You didn't say he drowned,' Russell said. 'I thought it was something else.' He was almost asleep, cheeks flushed, arms and legs flung out akimbo.

Maddy sat up and pushed the covers right off. The room was so hot. Through the window, orange stripes of headlights and street lights bent into the room. She still wasn't used to the strange patterns the lights made as they swung across the bed and the wardrobe. 'I don't know, exactly,' she said. The wrecker had touched the side of his head carefully, moved his hair aside to show her a dark bruise.

'Know . . . exactly . . .' Russell mumbled, each word running into the other. He turned on to his stomach, reached out and held her ankle.

'You're going to sleep,' Maddy said, looking down at him, at the smooth curve of his back, at the freckles on his arms. He knew she didn't get to sleep easily. A few years ago, at the beginning, he would sing to her, low, quiet songs, his voice beautiful and unexpected. He used to pull the covers over them and sing.

The wrecker flailed out and something clattered on to the floor. His chest heaved and rattled.

'Russell?' Maddy said. She touched his warm shoulder, then lay back down. She pulled the covers over and then pushed them off again. What she wanted was for Russell to sing for her, something slow, something bluesy. Instead, he pulled up the sheet and went to sleep, his breathing turning slow and regular, leaving her marooned sleepless in the bed, half-imagining it was her fighting for breath, half-imagining the covers as a dark roof of water.

'We'll be glad to get rid of the place,' her father had said, running his hand over cracks that he couldn't afford to fix, disguising doubt with the stern, disapproving voice her mother hated. 'Should have done it years ago, I suppose.' The wind came in straight off the sea, beat branches against the house. A whole tree had fallen through a window one spring.

'I suppose so,' Maddy had said to him, already feeling lost, cast adrift. She'd thought her parents would live there for ever, and so had hardly been back in the five years since moving out. Whenever she'd packed her bags, hauled them between towns and flats, her old house was there in the background, solid, stable as a beacon.

The wind had whipped in harder, lifting tiles on the roof. 'It's the sound of angels running,' her father had once told her.

It was too hot to concentrate. The freezer groaned and laboured. Wave after wave of heat rolled in. Maddy put her feet in a bowl of cold water but it didn't help.

'Try to keep the windows open,' Russell told her, halfway out of the door. 'They were all shut when I got back yesterday.' He had started leaving for work earlier and earlier, pillow creases etched on to each cheek.

The wrecker was in the spare bedroom, muttering, sorting. The room had become a nest of his smells and noises – smoke, seaweed, the wind moving across water – and they seeped out into the rest of the flat, hung across it like low fog. Maddy was aware of every sound and movement, every box opening, every object lifted out and inspected. 'The windows,' she said finally, but Russell had already gone. She sat there, listening. Boxes opened, coins or marbles were tipped on to the floor, wood clacked against wood. She pushed the chair back and got up, went through the kitchen and down the hall, leaving behind a trail of wet footprints.

'The bird pictures,' she said. The wrecker was sorting through paintings of birds: jays, owls, woodpeckers, all with small heads and mean, staring eyes. She had never liked them, used to walk past them quickly if she was ever alone in the house.

'Gold in the frames,' he said.

Maddy nodded. She reached into one of the boxes and lifted out a bunch of keys. They were all different sizes and weights. There was one for each room and window, spares, a heavy key that didn't fit any locks in the house, a hotel key, kept for years and never thrown out. The key to her mother's diary, tiny as a leaf. 'Open it,' one of her friends had dared when they'd come across it, but Maddy couldn't bring herself to. She took each key off the ring, held them in her palm, laid them out in size order.

The wrecker looked at the keys carefully, then picked up the rustiest one. 'There's a town underwater,' he said. 'I've seen it. There's a whole town under there. Streets and houses and water and trees.'

'Where?' Maddy asked.

'A flood. Water everywhere. A whole town. Bubbles coming up out of chimneys.'

'Where?' she asked again.

The wrecker looked at her and shook his head. 'Doors and windows float away,' he said.

'He might have murdered people, Maddy,' Russell said quietly. The wrecker was in the living room. They could hear Grand Prix engines screeching round a track. 'You know what that lamp's for, don't you? For luring boats on to rocks. He will have robbed them. He's a thief. How do you know he isn't a murderer?' He traced the knots in the kitchen table, glanced towards the living room. He smelled sweet, of soap and sun cream.

'Only boats that were already wrecked,' Maddy said. The air in the flat was so thick it was difficult to take a breath.

'How do you know?'

'He told me. They were desperate. They were all poor.'

'When's he going to leave?' Russell asked. He leaned towards her and touched her hand. He had bitten all his nails. 'Maddy, I . . .'

The wrecker appeared suddenly in the kitchen. Water dripped off his clothes and on to the floor. He stared at them with his pale eyes.

Russell cleared his throat. 'Those are good boots, William. Where did you get them?'

'They're mine.' The wrecker walked over to the table and slumped down in a chair, sticking his legs right out. 'Prevailing winds, onshore, moon almost full, high tide in a few weeks,' he said. 'Water warming up by degrees. High pressure after high pressure.' He sighed loudly. 'Moon almost full.'

The washing machine drained with a loud gurgle and started to spin. The wrecker got up to look. The clothes were flinging themselves against the sides. He was following the spinning so intently that he pitched forwards, knocking a plate off the table and breaking it in half. 'This is a sinking ship,' he said, looking down at the plate.

Damp appeared on the walls. It crept up in slow increments, a line of seaweed marking its highest point. Maddy started to watch it, and every time she checked the water had risen, millimetre by millimetre.

* * *

There was a hose-pipe ban. A leaflet with advice for coping in a heat wave was delivered to every house. Water is essential, it said, stay hydrated.

Maddy put on her headphones and listened to her latest audio file. It was an interview with a group of women about what they liked to drink on a night out. 'Wine,' she typed. 'Cream.' She listened for noises coming from the spare bedroom. She couldn't hear the wrecker, she couldn't hear if the boxes were being opened. The door of her old house swung shut and locked behind her. The women talked over one another and laughed. Someone said they wanted to go and dance. There was a faint static buzzing underneath the voices. Maddy took the headphones off and adjusted them. The static got louder. The file leapt and peaked with noise.

A slow, deep voice started to speak over the interview. 'Visibility moderate or good, occasionally poor,' it said. 'Rain and drizzle and then fair.'

The wrecker walked through the kitchen and the voice got even louder. The women's voices were drowned out completely. 'Some squally showers,' the voice said. 'Wind north-westerly, three or four.'

The static hummed and then roared.

She struggled in her sleep, sinking deeper and then rising back up with a gasp, almost awake. Her sleep was flimsy, broken, as if someone was throwing stones into water. Minutes seemed like hours. Through the wall, the wrecker flailed and hacked up salt.

'Huh?' Maddy said. 'What?' She turned on to one side and then the other. Russell's body was too warm so she lifted his arm, rolled away from him and lay at the edge of the bed.

Light from the wrecker's lamp spilled under the door. Shapes bled into one another, grew. The walls shifted. She could hear noises from downstairs: voices, footsteps, someone laughed, a door opened and closed, outside the window a magnolia tree creaked. The sea rolled over and over.

In the morning, she didn't know where she was, or, for a second, who she was lying next to.

Another meeting to type. 'Management,' Maddy wrote. 'We'll go under if this doesn't work.' Her eyes felt tired, heavy. Static droned in the background but she carried on typing. She followed the rhythm of the voices, the static washing over her.

After a while, she noticed that the recording had stopped. She took her hands off the keyboard and looked over what she'd written.

'Viking: visibility moderate to poor. Prevailing winds, moon almost full. Water warming up by degrees. Virgo, Pisces, the little bear. What are they saying on that ship? Two to three, three to four, four to five. Some squally showers. Footprints across the beach. The highest tide in centuries.'

It went on and on for pages. Maddy read it twice then played the recording again. It spoke of tides and empty beaches, of the wind finding ways through solid rock. Maddy could feel herself standing on an empty beach, cold sand under her feet, nothing but water in front of her. She was still listening to it when Russell came in. He put his cool hands on her shoulders. 'Sea state calm,' she told him.

Every day, as soon as Russell left for work, Maddy would go into the spare room. The boxes would be open, the wrecker muttering and sifting through them. She would open books, scan the pages, run her finger along pictures and spines swollen with damp.

'Once upon a time,' the wrecker would murmur, his voice hollow and mournful.

She would take out paper flowers, board games, hairpins, and lay them out on the carpet in rows. Her mother had collected jars of buttons and Maddy would tip them out and divide them into piles by colour, by shape. She wound and rewound a clock. She took photos out of albums, studied each one, and then carefully slotted them back inside the crinkled plastic. The house aged in each picture – it began to fade, cracks appeared, the roof warped, roots dug themselves into foundations.

She would unfold the threadbare, dusty clothes that she used to dress up in: a crocheted shawl, a fur hat, waders, high heels. She would unwrap jewellery from tissue paper, sort through drill bits and nails. She would look over address books, recipes, newspaper clippings.

The wrecker stacked up lampshades and crockery. 'Could do with a drink,' he would say. 'A lot to get through and the water's coming.'

Minutes turned into hours. When all the boxes were empty, Maddy would pack them up again, collecting everything together, closing the lids up tight. She would sigh, stay sitting among the boxes. Sand piled up in drifts.

'False lights,' the wrecker said, leaning out of the window. He polished his lamp and watched as the sky turned dark blue and other lights appeared, one by one, in the distance. Damp, humid air clamoured around him like birds.

\* \* \*

Stones appeared: grey and purple, some with dark veins, some speck-led with silver. Pebbles snaked down the hall; there were six smooth stones huddled in the corner of the bathroom, more inside cupboards. Tiny shells came out of the taps and filled the sink.

'Jesus, Maddy,' Russell said when he got in from work. He put his bag down and went over to the table. The wrecker had dragged stones across it and there were faint scratches in rings. 'Why didn't you stop him? You've been here all day.' He licked his finger and tried to rub out the scratches.

'I didn't notice,' Maddy said. She looked over at the table, at Russell. What was it the wrecker had told her? Something about wading out to sea, listening to crews talking on the trawlers and oil tankers that passed by. He heard them talking in Portuguese, Norwegian.

'How could you not notice?' Russell said. 'He would have dragged them right past you.' He picked up a stone and dropped it on the floor.

'It's not worth anything,' the wrecker said, glancing at the table. Maddy could hear waves rolling over and seagulls cawing inside his throat.

'I didn't notice,' she said again. She started to get up, to go over to Russell, but there was a heap of stones in her lap. She picked one up; it was cold and fitted perfectly in her hand.

Russell pushed the stones on to the floor. He kicked over the pile of stones in the bathroom. He picked up armfuls of them and took them outside.

Next morning, they were all back in exactly the same places.

'Prevailing winds, new moon,' the wrecker said. 'Temperatures rising.' Sand heaped under the table and the bed. The damp mark rose on the walls.

'You should get out of the house,' Russell told Maddy. 'When did you last go out?'

'I'm fine,' she said.

'Come on,' he said. 'We need to get out.'

'Another time.' She sifted through the sand with her fingers.


The news reported that the heat wave could break in the next few days. The wrecker shook his head. 'More high pressure,' he said.


No sound from the kitchen. The door was closed. The wrecking light shone faintly underneath and, now and again, it flashed and darkened as the wrecker paced in front of it.

Russell's favourite film was playing. 'Sit like this,' he said to Maddy. He pulled her towards him so she was leaning against his chest. She could feel his heartbeat. It was fluttery and fast and she pressed her ear against it. From there, she could see the water mark on the wall. It had risen again. She needed to watch it, keep a closer eye on it. It always rose the moment she looked away.

Russell shifted on the sofa and kept glancing at the kitchen door. 'What's he doing in there?' he said. 'I missed that bit. Have they found out where the killer is?' He leaned forwards, fixed his eyes on the TV. A man was being followed down a dark street. He stopped to light a cigarette. He carried on walking and his footsteps rang out on the pavement. The person behind got closer. He was carrying a gun.

Maybe the damp is rising right now, Maddy thought. She looked over quickly but the line hadn't moved.

The man with the gun raised his arm.

There was a crash and a sizzling, spitting noise from the kitchen. Acrid smoke swept into the room.

'Shit,' Russell said. He jumped up and pulled open the kitchen door.

'Heat rising and converging,' the wrecker said. He was hunched over the gas flame holding a charred gull's feather. Smoke poured off it. The alarm started its piercing wail.

Russell reached forwards and switched off the flame. He opened the window as wide as it would go and fanned the smoke out but it stayed where it was, hovering at waist height. 'You need to leave,' he said.

The wrecker stared at the place where the flame had been. 'The moon has craters and seas,' he said. 'Plato, Copernicus, Mare Crisium.' He smiled slowly.

Russell took a step towards him. 'You need to leave,' he said.

The wrecker smiled again. There was a quiet pop and the lights went out. The alarm stopped. The TV went blank. The fridge and freezer shuddered and ground to a halt. Silence spread over the flat. Outside, the street lamps were all still on and there were lights in other windows. The wrecker's lamp flickered, didn't cast any shadows.

Maddy leaned against the door frame. She was used to power cuts. They always used to have them. Her parents would get out candles and wind-up torches. The house would be scary at first, all dark spaces to cross and places for things to hide. Once, she heard her parents arguing, maybe she heard a plate hit a wall, but all that was forgotten – the house would glow, creak, rock her to sleep.

The silence deepened and spread. Russell paced in the bedroom. At 3 a.m. the wrecker's heavy footsteps moved through the flat. He sat on the sofa and the TV and lights clicked on quietly.

*    *    *

The damp mark rose halfway to the ceiling. Water gathered behind the walls, making them buckle like tired knees.

'This place hasn't got any weather,' the wrecker said. 'Where's all the mist blowing in? Where's all the sea mist?' He looked in the boxes. 'Where's all the water?'

Hours passed like minutes and Maddy hardly noticed. 'Look,' she said to the wrecker, 'painted plates.'

He looked at them with his pale eyes. 'Moon almost full,' he said, nodding.


The front door opened and Russell came in quietly and went straight into the bedroom. The wardrobe creaked. He went into the bathroom and came back out holding soap and his toothbrush. Maddy watched as he packed up a bag.

'I can't put it off,' Russell said, not meeting her eyes. 'Mike phoned me at work, asked if I could come and stay. They've got the new baby now.' He put socks in the bag, a torch, a book, a jumper. He packed as if he were nine years old, running away from home for the first time. Her heart felt damp and tired.

'OK,' she said. Russell wasn't allowed to take phone calls at work. The thought came from a long way away; she hardly noticed it. She went into the kitchen and made him a sandwich to take.

'Thanks,' Russell said. He packed it carefully. 'They've given me next week off.'

'OK,' Maddy said.

'I'll ring you,' Russell told her. He paused halfway through the door, then closed it quietly behind him.

After he had left, she walked slowly around the flat. She touched the walls and the windows and the doors. They were all damp. She left a handprint in the wet window.

'Full moon,' the wrecker said. He pointed at the sky. The moon hung there like a floating leaf. 'Those waves,' he said. 'Those tides.' He stared out of the window. He ran a feather along the sill.

Later, every noise Maddy heard became the front door opening, but it didn't open. She lay awake. Through the wall, the wrecker drowned again, over and over and over.

The town swayed in the heat. Afternoons turned to dark blue dusk. 'False lights,' the wrecker said.

The boxes were packed and unpacked. Tools, saucepans, candles, her father's old records, scratched and battered. Bird paintings, keys. The waxy smell of potpourri, the mustiness of cushions.

Sometimes the phone rang, but it cut off just before she could get to it.

At night, her old house loomed like a shipwreck. The bare whale-bones of the kitchen. Doors and cupboards floated out of the dark. Things shifted – if she walked into one hallway, she ended up in another. They stretched forwards without ending. One stairway became another stairway – front doors switched and opened out on to a porch, a street full of cars, a garden, miles and miles of water.

A bundle of letters. The wrecker rifled through them, the dry pages rustling and then sticking together under his damp fingers. 'Not worth anything,' he said. 'No good.' He threw them aside, picked up the glass vase, tested its weight and put it on the biggest pile. 'That bit, not that bit,' he said, going back over shoes and beads.

Maddy picked the letters up. Her grandmother's writing, her cousin's. The pages were brown and thin, well-thumbed. Slotted in the middle, almost hidden, were different letters, typed, addressed to her mother. Maddy read them over. She read them again. She put them back in the box.

The wrecker paced around the flat. 'Cumulus and cirrus,' he said. He started to swing his lamp in the window, slowly, for hours.

Another dream: her old house floated upwards on currents of air like a bird. Bricks and stone piled up and then toppled and crashed down and she woke up expecting to see bricks all around her.

The carpet in the hall was soaking. Her feet sunk in and left dents that slowly filled, as if it were a mire or quicksand. Water pooled in the doorway of the spare bedroom. The door frame dripped. The boxes looked darker, their sides bulged and warped.

The wrecker was pacing around the room. 'Where am I?' he asked. 'Where's all the water?'

Maddy opened the lids and wet cardboard tore off in her hand. The smell of wet cardboard. The smell of wet paper and wool. She looked inside the boxes. They were full of sand and water. Paper was soaked through and torn. Keys had rusted. Sand had worked its way behind the glass of clocks and packed itself into jars. A box gave way and split and water spilled over her feet.

'What have you done?' she asked the wrecker.

The wrecker paced and paced. 'There's a whole town underwater,' he said.

'My things,' Maddy said. 'Everything.'

He sat down. Water sloshed over the tops of his boots. 'There was a flood. No one knew it was going to happen. Houses and trees underwater.'

Maddy knelt down and scooped sand out of the boxes. There was too much of it and eventually she gave up, let it trickle over her feet.

'It's not worth anything,' the wrecker told her, staring out of the window.


Maddy opened the front door and stepped out on to the street. The light hurt her eyes and she blinked, once, twice. She couldn't remember the last time she had been out. Her key felt strange in her hand. The front steps were overgrown with wilted yellow flowers; the grass had turned brown and dry. There was a strange hush, as if things had been paused, suspended.

Her car was coated in dust and pollen. Inside, plastic on the dashboard had melted and solidified in small ripples. She drove out of town. A breeze came in through the window, cooler perhaps, thinner. It picked up as she got nearer the sea and the roads opened out. 'Beware crosswinds,' a sign said. Her mother used to think they'd be pushed right off the cliff. She used to lean her body the other way, against the wind, as if to balance them out.

It was early evening when she got there. The moon was already out. She saw the chimney of the house first, rising up from behind the hill, and then she turned a corner and there was the sea, laid out flat in front of her. Everything was so familiar that she seemed to see the chimney, the sea, a moment before they actually appeared – and so as she drove, the landscape echoed, repeated itself, like somebody who was old or lonely.

She turned down the lane that led to the house, the car bumping and sinking into potholes. She stopped in front of the gate. She had expected the house to be ramshackle by now, half wild. She thought the wind would have found its way into it, making the holes and cracks wider, buckling the roof. She had imagined the magnolia pushing its way through the windows. But the house was newly painted, reinforced, the roof had been fixed and there were different tiles on it. It looked strong, storm-proof. She got out of the car, a few goosebumps on her arms. The wrecker's voice clamoured for attention in her ear but she pushed it aside and it became nothing more than a seagull cawing above her.

There was a child swinging on the gate. She stared at Maddy. She had a sequined evening dress on, so big it slipped down over her chest. She clutched the gate with bare sandy feet. 'Who are you?' she asked.

'There used to be a magnolia,' Maddy said. 'By that window.'

'You mean the lantern tree? It got cut down. I cried, although Dad said I shouldn't.'

'Cut down.'

'He said it creaked too much. He said it would keep me awake. He's scared of storms, I think. Why's there pollen all over your car?' She kicked at the wood, wiped sand off her cheek.

'I used to live here,' Maddy told her.

The girl narrowed her eyes to stones. She swung harder, looked back at the house. 'I'm late for my party,' she said, although she didn't climb down off the gate.

Maddy stood in the street, looking up. There was no light in her kitchen window. No flame flickered out through the glass. A cool breeze caught her hair and moved on. The house was dark. There were pebbles scattered over the pavement and in the front garden. She felt like she was returning from a long way away. She could hear the phone ringing from inside. 'Where have you been?' Russell would ask her when they spoke, his voice fragile and graceful as a bird. The house was dark and quiet. She would lean into the phone, hold it as close as she could to her ear, the connection brief and distant, but she would grasp it as she would a hand reaching down through water.

The street was hushed. Someone had tied a balloon to their front door and it strained against its string, trying, always, to lift away.

The phone rang again. She walked into the dark house.

# Magpies

*Be wary of the solitary magpie – don't listen to a word it says.*

I WAS DRIVING HOME. The sky was dark blue and the trees along the road, all bent in one direction, looked like the silhouettes of fishermen leaning over water. I was taking the longer route back. The road wound up high and everything around it was bare and wind-battered. Whatever the weather was, you knew about it up there, and it could change quickly, too. You could be driving along and suddenly there would be clouds and then rain when there hadn't been any clouds before. Sleet could roll in. I swear that I once saw forked lightning on a still, blue day. Each flash was so bright I saw them for hours after, stamped on the kitchen walls and in the bathroom mirror.

I wound the window down, let in the cool air. I was thinking about these dreams my wife had been having. It had got to the point where every night she would dream about the last thing I'd talked about. So I mention the crack in the stairs and she dreams of me walking up a staircase and out through the roof. I mention the rust on my bike wheel and she dreams of fairgrounds, the smell of them, the clank of metal and lights in the distance. It was getting to me but I didn't know why. I kept thinking about it and I kept thinking I wouldn't say anything that she could possibly dream about, but then she'd ask me questions, get me talking about something or other, and straight away I'd forget.

I'd just been to see Mae. She was back in town for a few days and we'd met at Herb's, the roadside café we always used to go to. I still go there a lot, sometimes with a couple of guys after work, sometimes by myself. There's usually someone you can get talking to – Herb, people travelling on business, long-haul drivers.

I sat at a table in the corner and waited. There was the usual smell of vinegar and coffee and frying. Herb's classical music playing in the kitchen. Pictures of horse-racing and framed newspaper clippings about local disasters. I loved the place. It felt like things could happen there, anyone could be passing through. It was pretty empty that evening, just one other guy by the door, a motorbike helmet on the table next to him. He reminded me of the time I'd seen what I thought was a horrific motorbike crash. I'd pulled over, shaking, gone up to the pieces of metal and helmet strewn across the road, but it was all brand new, with warehouse labels stuck on from where they'd fallen off the back of a lorry.

I changed gear and thought about what Mae had said about it being four years since she'd last seen me. I was sure it was only two – I didn't realise time had gone that fast. I opened the window a little wider; there was a good breeze. My skin felt warm and clammy. Time must be going faster than I thought. I was thinking about that, trying to recollect what I'd done in the last few years, when something banged hard into the car.

'What the devil?' I said, which is what I always say when something surprises me. I'd rather swear like anybody else but I can't shift it – my granddad says it and the words have stuck to me like burrs. I pulled over but I didn't really think I'd hit anything. Maybe I saw a flash at the last minute, something black, some kind of movement, but I thought it was a stone at most. I turned the engine off, got out, and looked under the wheels. There were other tyre marks, a few stones, but nothing else. Something pale caught my eye but it was just sheep's wool tangled in the hedge.

I was about to get back in the car when I heard rustling further up the road. I hesitated for a second, then craned forwards, but the light coming from inside the car made everything else too dark. I closed the door and the light went out. There was a black and white feather in the road. It had a sheen to it, blue, maybe some purple. Further along, at the bottom of the low hedge, there were more feathers, a heap of feathers, which turned out to be a magpie that I'd hit with the wing mirror.

I stood still. I didn't go any closer. A car went past, its lights picking out the road, a tree, and then making everything seem darker and closer again.

The bird shifted and raised its head up. One of its wings was hanging like a broken umbrella. I didn't go any closer but I couldn't stop looking at its wing. The magpie lifted it up then let it fall back on to the road. I heard the feathers brush against the tarmac; I thought I heard a faint snap, as if someone had stepped on a branch in a wood.

After a while, the magpie heaved itself up so it was standing. It looked ragged and unsteady. I wanted to say something to it, that I was sorry, I guess, that I was really sorry. 'Birds don't fly in the dark,' I said instead. I hadn't paid much attention at school but I knew most birds didn't fly around once it got dark. 'Birds aren't meant to fly in the dark,' I told the magpie. It came out sounding like an accusation. But what was it doing flying around in the dark?

The magpie's eyes shifted but I couldn't tell where it was looking.

I looked away. I did that thing where you go 'brrr' and skip around on the ground if you get cold, hands clasped like you're praying and running at the same time. It wasn't even that cold, just a chill in the air that meant autumn was coming. I glanced back at the car, thought I heard another engine, but there was nothing. I heard something else.

'What did you say?' My voice was loud and sudden, disturbing the emptiness and the quiet. But the magpie had said something, I was sure. It tilted its head. The hedge was full of broom and the grey pods, like cocoons, kept swaying and shivering. I took a step closer. An image came into my head of the china clay tips I had to drive past on the way to work. They looked so desolate. They looked like mountains covered in snow but they weren't mountains. I had always felt it was some kind of trick, the fact that they looked so much like mountains when, really, I was on the same flat ground as always.

'What did you say?' I asked.

It had sounded like, 'This old place.' I could hardly catch it. Maybe it hadn't said anything, maybe it was just its feathers brushing against the road.

'This old place again.' Those were the first words Mae said when she walked into Herb's and sat down opposite me. She looked the same, except that she'd cut off all her long hair, which made her face seem thinner, more severe, older than twenty-six. Her eyes were different colours: one blue, one grey – I'd actually forgotten about that, forgotten that she used to say things like, 'I'm indecisive, can't you tell?' and point at them.

She ordered coffee and glanced around the café. 'I can't believe we used to come here all the time,' she said. 'Why did we?'

I shrugged. 'We liked it.'

'I remember it being bigger. I don't remember it like this.'

The lights in there were dim and one flickered on and off. The plastic tables were stained and buckled; there was a crack down one window. From the kitchen, Herb bellowed along to a violin, his voice rich and scratchy.

'Mum's turned my bedroom into a study since I last visited,' Mae said. 'I have to sleep on the sofa.' Her foot danced up and down with the music; I knew that she was already desperate to leave town, already thinking of the journey back.

'My room's exactly the same,' I told her. 'I went round there the other day and found all those badges I used to collect. They were piled up in a drawer.'

'You gave me one,' Mae said. 'It had a clown on or something.'

'Have you still got it?' I asked her.

The guy with the motorbike helmet stood up and walked to the bathroom, knocking into chairs on his way. 'Excuse me, excuse me,' he kept saying to the chairs.

Mae watched him, sighed. 'We should have gone somewhere else,' she said. She sipped her coffee without really drinking any. We used to like Herb's cheap, bitter coffee.

I put a sugar cube in for her and stirred it.

Silence on the road. An offshore wind picked up and swept in some clouds. I wanted to know what the magpie had said. I waited, but it didn't speak again. Instead, it started to move along the verge, slowly, very slow. It tried to lift itself into the air, then it fell back on to the road, sideways. It dragged itself up and half stumbled, half hopped two steps forward. Then it tried to lift itself into the air again and the whole thing started from the beginning. It looked like a dead leaf skidding along the road. I didn't want to watch the magpie struggling to move like that, but I did watch it.

After a few metres, it turned to the left and disappeared. The hedge was low and sharp. I didn't hear the magpie pushing through it. I waited awhile. I watched the empty space where the magpie had been. Another car went past behind me but I didn't turn round. The magpie's words edged and circled in my mind.

I went up to the hedge and saw that there was a small metal gate. The magpie had squeezed under it. It was the sort of gate you would hardly notice; in fact, I've driven that road since and I manage to miss it every time. Beyond the gate there was a flat scrubby field with nothing in it except a few dark trees at the end. The magpie started to move across the grass.

I should have been home by now. I wanted to be home. Right then, my wife would have been sitting at the kitchen table reading, a mug of lemon tea in front of her, her hair damp and frizzy from the bath she'd just had. I could smell the lemon, her damp hair. I could picture the light from our kitchen window, how it would look from outside as I paused just before the door, wisteria climbing all over the walls.

I climbed over the gate. The metal hummed when I jumped off it. I followed the magpie. Now and then, I would pass small white feathers that curled up like burnt paper. I could hardly see the magpie itself, so I just followed those white feathers.

Another feather and then another. The magpie was already halfway across the field so that, in the dark, it was almost out of my line of vision. It seemed to be moving so slowly, it seemed to be struggling, but whenever I glanced away and then looked back again, it had moved further forwards, widening the gap. It was impossible to catch up with it. I imagined pain shooting through with each step, I imagined bone rubbing against bone, but at the same time I was trying to work out what the magpie had said. Was it something about the road? Was it actually something about the road?

I heard that noise again, the voice. I almost caught it that time. It moved quietly along the grass. It was as if the magpie was speaking from behind a door, or its voice was coming from a long hallway that I couldn't see. There was a kid I used to know at school who said that he saw words as colours. He heard 'fish' and he saw gold flash and then ebb away. He heard 'chair' and there was a deep, calm green. I never understood what he meant before and I still don't really, but when I think of the magpie speaking, it reminds me of him every time. The magpie spoke and maybe I saw a face, blurry and indistinct, beckoning on the other side of a road.


'Where are you working now?' Mae asked me.

The guy with the motorbike had left and we were the only ones in there.

'Same place,' I said. 'I've started doing the orders.' I work at the ice cream factory, have done for seven years. It was only meant to be a casual job for one summer but it's close to where I live, and the work's easy once you know what you're doing.

'I'm in between,' Mae said. 'I was temping on reception at a dentist's.'

'You hate the dentist.'

'Yeah. I could hear drilling all the time. Apparently I started grinding my teeth at night.' She glanced down at her hands, then back up at me. She bit at her lip. She used to bite her lips till they bled. 'I could be anywhere next. An office, catering,' she said.

'Do you want more coffee?' I asked. 'I'm getting one.' I got up and went to the kitchen to ask Herb for more coffee. My mouth was dry.

He filled up two more cups, told me that he'd got one of those new grills I'd been telling him about. 'You fold the top down like this,' he said.

'It looks good.' I showed him how to work the timer.

'They finally sent it,' Herb said. He took an envelope out of his pocket and tipped a tiny green sliver on to his palm. A few months ago, someone had phoned him up and told him he'd won an emerald in a prize draw; all he had to do was send some money for postage. He'd been waiting every day for it. 'Turned out to be a scam,' he said. 'I knew it would be.' He'd been going on about it for so long he'd ended up getting both of our hopes up.

'Those things are always a scam,' I told him. The green chip was so small I could barely see it in his hand. I took the cups back in. 'I got you more coffee,' I said to Mae.

'Thanks.' She pulled the cup towards her, slopping coffee over the edge. 'Do you know that joke about the cat and the saucer?' she said.

I shook my head. I could smell strawberries on my clothes from work.

'A cat goes up to its saucer and finds a delicious piece of meat on it. The cat eats it and goes away. Later, it comes back and there's a big piece of fish. It eats that and goes away again.'

I watched her speaking, her small mouth, frown marks at the top of her nose, her voice slow. At school we'd told jokes all the time, thinking each one wise and magnificent.

'It has a wash, it has a nap, then it goes back to its saucer.' She stopped talking suddenly, her eyes wide, surprised. 'I forgot how it ends,' she said, almost smiling, the frown lines deepening.

\* \* \*

The field was blue-tinged, everything around had a blue to it. The magpie blended into the dark. My eyes ached as I tried to see where it was going. The grass underfoot was dry and crunchy, as if it was covered in frost but there wasn't a frost. There were thistles, spearing their way up through the ground. There were mushrooms too, fat and white and leaning out of the dark. The landscape was bare and open. One or two small lights from distant bungalows. I was so close to town and the sea was over there somewhere, but it felt like there was nothing near me, only this field and the magpie and the trees in the distance.

As I got closer to them, the trees stretched outwards and multiplied. I thought there were only a few of them, but now they thickened and spread backwards, gathering up the dark and the quiet. More clouds swept in and I started to zip up my jacket. I noticed that I was missing a couple of buttons off my shirt. There were gaps where the buttons should have been, but there weren't any frayed threads.

The magpie moved forwards without pausing. I tried to focus on it. I looked down at my missing buttons, and just at that moment, the magpie disappeared into the wood.

The pine trees smelled like soap and cold air. I ducked under a low branch and then stepped over another. I could hardly see anything and kept tripping over roots and stones. There were roots everywhere. They looked like they were grabbing handfuls of earth and pulling them upwards.

I followed the magpie and the small white feathers. After a while, it stopped and I stopped, too. There it was again, the magpie's voice, whispering. The rhythm of the words – what did they remind me of? Maybe the roots, weaving across the floor of the wood, all tangled up with each other. I saw myself tangled up in them, rooted to the spot.

\*   \*   \*

The door opened and a middle-aged couple came in. The bell on the door used to chime but now it makes a tinny thud. They sat at a table in the opposite corner to us. After a while, Herb came over and I heard them order tea and toast. Once Herb had brought it over, the woman took out a small pot of jam from her bag and started to spread it on the toast and cut it into triangles. They looked tired.

'I can't stay late,' Mae said.

Our coffee had gone cold by now and we had pushed it to one side. I'd crumbled a sugar cube over the table without noticing, and I started making patterns in the grains with my finger. 'Have you heard from Si?' I asked. 'Or Ruth and Pear?'

'A bit,' she said. 'Have you?'

'They haven't been back.'

'I bumped into your dad,' Mae said. She moved her legs out from under the table. She never liked to be in small spaces, always had to take the stairs rather than a lift. 'I forgot to tell you. Outside the optician's.'

'He thinks he's going blind.'

'He said that. He said he gets you to drive him places, and read out bits of the paper.'

'He's not going blind,' I said. I noticed that the couple in the corner were both leaning forwards over their table, talking in low voices. I wondered what they were saying. The man reached over and brushed crumbs off the woman's cheek.

Mae checked her watch, then touched the sleeve of her coat. Herb's music rang out from the kitchen.

'Time to go,' she said. She got her car keys out of her bag; same old bottle-opener key ring. She stood up and put on her coat.

The kitchen door swung open and Herb made his way over to our table. 'The grill's doing something funny,' he said to me. 'There's a red light. It won't cool down.'

'In a second,' I told him.

'Something's smoking on it,' Herb said.

'I'll leave you to it,' Mae told me. She tucked her chair under the table and said goodbye, said that she'd be back again sometime soon.

I watched her go, then turned to Herb and went to check the grill.

The trees were leaning in and dark all around. There was no sound except a faint wheezing which I thought was me but was actually the magpie breathing. It sounded like a struggle. I stood very still and listened to it, and to the wind finding its way through the trees.

The magpie kept tilting its head up towards a tree. After a while, it flapped its wings and rose about a foot off the ground. Its broken wing stayed locked to its side.

I moved forwards. The magpie flapped again, lifted itself up, then fell back, like a sheet of newspaper caught in a breeze. I thought about picking it up and putting it in the tree. I imagined holding it in my hands. I imagined its strange weight, its smoothness. The feathers would be smooth, but they would rasp against my hands, I was sure. I imagined its fluttery heartbeat. I didn't go any closer. But all the time I was standing there, I felt feathers against my hands and my wrists as if I had picked the magpie up.

I looked down at my feet and noticed that all the metal eyelets from my trainers had disappeared.

The magpie had stopped looking at the tree. It tucked its head down into its chest and crouched on the ground. I stood there and wondered what the magpie would do next. I could still feel its feathers on my hands. I brushed my fingers, trying to get rid of them. The trees crowded in and I couldn't tell which way we had come into the wood. The trees all looked the same, crowding in like that, but I just stood there, watching the magpie, and didn't look for the way out.

'What the devil,' the magpie whispered, or it may have just been the wind finding its way through the trees.

Something silver caught my eye. There was a dull glint on the ground further into the wood. I walked past the magpie and sifted through pine needles. I found a set of keys, and they were my keys. My key ring was on them. My heart beat a little faster. I checked my pockets to make sure they were definitely mine. I hadn't even been this far into the wood. My pockets were empty. I put the keys back in my pocket and zipped it up tight.

From where I was now, I could see a shape in the trees. At first, it looked like another tree that was leaning out at a strange angle, but then I saw that it was a triangle made up of thick branches. They were all leaning into the middle, like a tepee, and were tied together with rope. It was some kind of den. It blended into the trees so well that it was almost impossible to see. Scanning your eyes across the wood, it would be easy to miss it completely.

I walked towards the den. There were a few trees with low branches that looked good for climbing. I used to climb trees all the time. Beech trees were best. When I was younger, I used to climb into a beech and stay there all day, sometimes into the night. I liked to go right into the middle so there were leaves above and below me. Sometimes, I'd go to sleep and wake up thinking I was in bed and wondering where all the walls had gone. I hadn't climbed a tree in a long time. I stepped on to one of the pine's low branches. It bent and swayed under my body. I took another step up, then another. The branches were thin and I knew, just as I was putting my foot on the next one, that it wouldn't take my weight. I grabbed handfuls of pine needles and air on my way down.

I landed on my knees. The smell of damp earth and old leaves. When I got up, I looked back at the magpie. It had been watching me the whole time, its head tilted to one side. I could see its small chest heaving up and down, but its eyes were focused and still.

I ducked my head into the den. There were a few sweet wrappers glinting silver, pine needles everywhere, an old blanket and a mug. The ground was smooth, footprintless. The entrance was small but I stooped down and squeezed in, bumping my shoulders and the sides of my arms against the wood. Further in, I saw my buttons, and the eyelets from my trainers, and three small badges piled up in the corner.

I sat cross-legged in the middle of the den, my knees touching the sides. I looked out of the triangular doorway. It crossed my mind that I could light a fire; I knew how to do it. I pictured myself from far away: the den, a fire outside in the middle of all these trees, a thin thread of smoke rising, but I didn't light one. I just sat there and a nice chill made its way inside the den and through my skin.

I don't know how much time passed. Part of me wanted to get up and drive back home, part of me wanted to go in the opposite direction – I didn't know where. I stayed sitting where I was, in between. I thought about the other lives I could have had. I thought about home. I didn't get up. I touched my pocket to make sure my keys were still there.

Rain was gathering. There was a soft flapping and scuffling and I heard the magpie moving past the den. I heard it breathing. I could feel its feathers on my wrists and arms. It moved through the pine needles and, after a while, the sound got fainter. I didn't know how far it would be able to go until it had to stop for the last time. I listened to the magpie going further and deeper into the trees, and it was as if I was following it – it was as if I was going further and deeper into the trees. I could feel myself brushing past branches and roots. I could see the shadows between the trees and the dark and the stillness.

I would go back soon. I would pause before the front door and see the wisteria climbing all over the walls. I would climb into the warm bed. I would feel my wife's soft skin. She would ask where I had been. I knew that I wouldn't tell her about the magpie. I wouldn't tell her about following it through the field and into the wood. Because I also knew this: if I told her, she would dream about it, and in the morning I would wake up and see her looking at me strangely, and I would find out that she'd dreamed of me dragging pine trees through the front door of the house, needles carpeting the floors, or that she'd dreamed me half-magpie, black and white feathers on my neck and arms, and that she'd woken up seeing feathers scattered across the room.

# The Giant's Boneyard

Nothing moved across the moor except the rain, which appeared as suddenly and soundlessly as a face pressed against a window. Summer was almost over. A low sheet of cloud had appeared one morning at the beginning of August and never left, its bright greys worrying at the skyline. The sun lingered behind it and didn't break out. The muggy heat dropped and chilled at night and gathered again in the morning. People ate ice creams with the smell of bonfires in the air, fat bluebottles knocking into their bare arms.

Gog tried to curl himself up more tightly under the tarpaulin but his phantom body still sprawled out into the rain. His arms and legs felt soaking, the wispy hair on them plastered down in dark straggles. Wet grass brushed against his fingers and his calf was pressed against a stone. His real body (average height for a twelve-year-old boy according to the NHS website) was still dry, still staggeringly close to Sunshine. But he could feel the faint prickle of grass rash stippling his wrists and midges biting his ankles. Gog hated midges. He hated being in small spaces like this: it made him more aware of his phantom body than ever. This summer it had definitely become more intense – he could feel it surrounding him pretty much all the time now and it was getting difficult to ignore.

He and Sunshine had crawled into the den to escape getting drenched. At the beginning of summer, when they first started coming up here, they wouldn't have bothered avoiding the rain. But now they were acting more quietly, more carefully. It was like all their movements had become slower and more deliberate. Gog knew something had changed but he couldn't tell exactly what it was. All he knew was that he and Sunshine were now people who watched, rather than played in, the rain. And he also knew that however tired or bored they got hanging around together all day every day, they would carry on doing it until the summer ended, repeating the same conversations and jokes over and over without properly listening to them any more.

They couldn't keep away from the boneyard either. They would start walking and messing around and end up out there without even thinking about it. The boneyard was on the edge of the moor. A faint trail, overgrown with gorse and heather, led out to it from town. No one knew how or why it was there, just that it had always been there and always would be. Hardly anyone came out to visit it, not even the handful of stray giants who were rumoured to wander around the wilder areas of the moors and cliffs. Kids sometimes came to loaf around but there was the skate park and the fountain, which were closer. Adults would visit, huddle dwarfed and shivering under the bones and not come back.

There were hundreds of bones, heaped and leaning like the beams and joints of an abandoned mansion. They were spread over an area of damp moorland the size of two football fields and they changed that flat landscape into a petrified forest. Tibiae, fibulas and hips tangled together. Shoulder blades sprawled like torn-off car doors. Femurs leaned out from the ground as if a giant had died standing up and collapsed around his own legs. Sternums and collarbones piled up, jaws bit at the ground like old animal traps, and kneecaps mushroomed from the grass.

Gog was afraid of it, in awe of it, drawn to it. He ran his hands along the bones, testing the size and weight of them. The NHS website said that 'although height is inherited, there may be incon-sistencies in families'. He quoted that to himself a lot while he was up there, especially when his chest went all tight and the bones seemed to stretch and grow and crowd around him. He was a pretty big inconsistency in his family: his father had been a giant and everyone was waiting for him to catch up. So far, all he'd got was a phantom body that confused him, tripped him up and sometimes made him over-arc when he went for a piss because he couldn't tell how far away he was from the toilet. There was nothing about phantom bodies on any websites or in any books. He figured it must be the first stage in the growth process but he wasn't entirely sure. He couldn't ask his dad because he'd never met him and he couldn't ask his mum because then she'd get her hopes up and he didn't want to disappoint her any more than he could help.

The den they'd found was a piece of tarpaulin someone had draped over dry branches and two rotting fence panels. It smelled weird in there, musty and smoky and old, like someone dead had just farted. Gog said that to Sunshine. 'It smells like a dead guy just farted in here.'

She rolled her eyes. Her cool bare arm was touching his. 'Get over it,' she told him, flicking hair out of her eyes. She looked up at the roof. 'Don't you love the sound of the rain hammering down like this?' she asked.

'I guess,' he said. He moved his foot so that it touched her sandal.

'What does it sound like to you? To me it sounds like something very sad is happening.'

Gog could feel his arse going numb. He shifted around. Sunshine always said things like that now, that 'something very sad was happening'. He wished she wouldn't. It was just rain; he didn't want rain to become more than that. 'I bet this is a murderer's hideout,' he said.

'There are no murderers up here,' Sunshine told him.

'Yeah, there are. That's what this smell is, I reckon. It's a body buried right underneath us.' He was always trying to freak Sunshine out.

'Actually, it would be the best place to do it,' she said. 'No one's going to notice a few extra bones around here.'

Gog hadn't thought of that. 'Exactly,' he said. He swallowed and checked around. Last year, there was that murdered body someone found in the reservoir, or was it a walker who'd slipped? He bumped his knee into Sunshine's. She sighed heavily. Her breath smelled sweet and bitter and dry, like toothpaste and peanut butter.

'There are no murderers.' She drew up her knees and hugged them with both arms. Gog felt the warmth from her leg evaporate. He could hear his watch ticking and wondered if Sunshine could too. He was meant to meet his mum in town in an hour.

'Your watch is righteously pissing me off,' Sunshine said. She lifted up a flap of the tarpaulin and peered out. The rain had stopped. She crawled out and Gog followed behind. Huge bones lay all around them like windblown birches. Some were piled haphazardly; others were laid out in weird patterns. Twelve spines, the vertebrae all intact, had been pressed into the ground in circles. There was a pyramid of skulls and a warped totem pole made from interlocking pelvis bones.

Sunshine tightrope-walked across a shin, her hands outstretched. The bones were slippery after the rain and she slid off on to the grass. She looked fine and hadn't fallen hard.

'Are you OK?' Gog asked, hurrying over not too quickly, not too slowly. Sometimes she liked his help and sometimes she didn't.

'Quit fussing,' she said, brushing her shorts. 'You are such a hypochondriac.' The first time she'd said that to him she'd called him a 'hypoallergenic' and he'd had to correct her. Even though it was a mistake, Sunshine telling him that he was unlikely to cause an allergic reaction was probably the best compliment he'd had so far from a girl. She walked over to a skull that had fallen off the top of the pyramid. It was the smallest skull there but was still as big as a television. A hairline crack inched up its left cheek. Gog had done some research and reckoned that a normal skull as old as these, which had been continuously exposed to air, would have shattered after a fall like that. It seemed like these bones weren't going anywhere; they were beyond breaking, erosion or decay.

'Check this out,' Sunshine said, sticking her fist through an eye socket and moving it around. All the skull's hollows were smoothed, wind-polished. Sometimes the wind whistled through the gaps in the bones so that it sounded as if they were singing mournfully. It reminded Gog of his mum singing along to her Joni Mitchell CD, her voice thin and wavering as she struggled with all the high notes.

Sunshine stood up and tried to push the skull but it didn't move. 'Piece of crap.' She looked at Gog then kicked at it, but not hard. She scrambled on to it and sat cross-legged on top. 'This one could be your dad,' she said, squinting up at him. Sometimes her laugh was small and hard. She always said something like that when they were around the bones, maybe to test him, and Gog always said the same thing back.

'Yeah, I think it probably is him actually. He says, can you move your fat ass off?' What he really wanted to say was that these bones were hundreds of years old and besides, his dad probably wasn't even dead. There was hardly any evidence. He kicked at the ground below her. 'Besides, he's probably not even dead,' he said quietly.

Sunshine had been humming loudly to herself but she stopped and looked up. 'How do you know, though?' she asked eagerly. 'How are you so sure?'

'I'm not sure exactly,' he said. 'Some things you think you just know.'

'Huh?'

'What I mean is, there are some things you think you just know. Do you know what I mean?' He couldn't describe it any better than that, the strong feeling he had. He could tell that Sunshine had been expecting him to say something else, that she didn't understand what he meant. He had failed. He'd had his chance to talk to her about it and he'd gone and screwed it up. He should have told her about the waxed jacket his dad had left behind in the hall, how it hung down like a greasy curtain and draped over the floor, except he didn't really know what he would have said about that either.

'Yeah,' Sunshine said, picking at a toenail. 'He probably just got sick of your mum.'

Something dropped into Gog's stomach. The sky was hard and bright and grey. The wet grass seeped into his canvas shoes. Sunshine didn't like his mum. She said that she had weird Freudian abandonment issues, whatever those were. He supposed it was fair to say that his mum was a little bit intense but it was only because she wanted the best for him. It wasn't like she did anything for herself. She never did anything for herself. She had always made sacrifices, a word which, to Gog, was tangled up with images of lambs and blood and crosses, and he couldn't untangle it now. She bought him protein shakes that were meant to increase his muscle mass. They tasted like strawberries and metal. He had a really fast metabolism, though, so they didn't help much; he stayed as scrawny as ever. She'd sent him on a caving holiday but he came back diagnosed with mild claustrophobia and still dreamed of rocks and dripping water. And she'd devised an exercise regime for him: ten minutes of hanging from a bar above his door to stretch out his spine plus another ten minutes of lifts and curls. He even stuck to it most of the time.

'Do you often just feel like breaking something?' she would ask, always on the lookout for flashes of anger, for the blank eyes and tension that come before violence.

'Sometimes,' he'd reply. 'But not that often.'

Then she would nod slowly and thoughtfully, a cup of tea going cold at her elbow.

Sunshine scrambled on to her feet and balanced on the skull's crown. 'Hey, give me a piggyback off here,' she said.

As Gog stood there, waiting for her to climb on to his back, he lurched forcefully back into his phantom body. His back felt about three feet higher than it actually was and he had to resist the urge to curl right over so that Sunshine could reach his shoulders. 'What are you doing?' she asked him.

'Nothing. Waiting for you.'

'You're hunching. Stop hunching.'

He straightened up and concentrated as hard as he could on his real body. Sunshine climbed on, wrapped her arms around his neck and her legs around his stomach. Gog stood there. He wasn't sure what he was meant to do now. Should he walk or run? Would he have to do that thing where you jig up and down, or was that just for little kids? Sunshine's warm chest was pressing into his back. He knew he had to keep concentrating as hard as he could so that he didn't do anything stupid like fall over or drop her. If he was standing on his phantom legs it meant that, logically, his real legs must be dangling in the air. It made him dizzy just thinking about it. Plus, Sunshine was actually a lot heavier than she looked. She seemed all slim and light when you saw her, but once she was on your back it was a completely different story. He locked his knees. Her hair was draped over his ears and cheeks and he had to keep blinking a strand out of his eye. He stood there stiffly and she clung on. A crow barked in the distance. Something rustled in the gorse. Sunshine shifted her weight. 'I think I'll get down now,' she said eventually, dropping a leg towards the floor. Her feet crunched down on teeth that were embedded in the soil like old confetti.

They looked down and scuffed at them with their shoes. There was the oniony smell of sweat. Nothing was ever as Gog expected it. The only party he'd ever been to was a let-down: half a flat beer and watching other people play computer games. He really ought to think about leaving soon. It would take fifteen minutes to walk back and his mum would definitely be on time; she would probably be early, looking disappointed that he'd kept her waiting. They were going to meet outside the church and then buy Gog's school stuff. They did the same thing every year. His mum called it their date and they had to go to the café for lunch and order things like croque monsieurs and bruschettas, his mum dabbing at the corners of her lips with a napkin even when there was nothing on them. And, shoved under the table, there would be bags of Aertex polo shirts and navy jumpers, all about three sizes too big, that he would have to try to swap with someone as soon as term started.

Sunshine picked up a bumpy knucklebone and cupped it in her palm. 'Hey Gog, go long,' she said, raising her arm. He started running backwards just as she dropped her hand and laughed at him. He stuffed his hands in his pockets and tried to turn his run into something else, a leap maybe, or a feint, as if he knew she was going to do that. It was so humid. It brought out the stinging feeling in the skin under his nose that would probably turn into more blackheads. 'You're such a retard,' Sunshine told him. But she said it affectionately; at least he thought she did. So he made a magnifying glass out of his hand, ran up to her and bent down over her shoes in his best Sherlock Holmes impression. Her toes were tiny. She'd painted the nails a deep purple.

'Ah, elementary, my dear Watson,' he said, grabbing her foot in his hand so that she had to wobble around on one leg. He rubbed over her ankle with his thumb and index finger. She jerked her foot away, laughed a little bit but not much.

'I hate that Columbo thing you do,' she told him.

There were chips all over the varnish when Gog saw it up close. The nail underneath looked pale and vulnerable. A few months ago, he'd walked in on his mum while she was getting dressed. He'd seen her thighs and they were strange, very white and puckered, and there were dark purple marks on them. He thought it must mean she was ill in some way but when he looked it up he couldn't find any symptoms that matched the description.

Sunshine was looking at him. Her eyes were very blue, like raspberry sours or the error screen that comes up when your computer dies. He probably loved her, after all, if love was this cold and lonely and sad. He should tell her. The summer was trailing away from them.

'It'll be shit when school starts,' he said. She slid her eyes away. That wasn't what she wanted. He jumped up and swiped at a moth, suddenly needing to do something. He was eight feet tall, four feet wide; he felt fence-shaped: flat and grey and going on for ever. The moth stuck to his palm in a soft brown crumple.

'What did you just do?' Sunshine asked. 'Did you just kill a moth?'

'No,' he said. He glanced at it then flicked it off. Shimmering dust filmed his skin. He covered the moth with his foot.

'Let me look at that.' Before he could stop her, Sunshine grabbed his hand and saw the marks.

'The encyclopaedia says that most moths only live about a week anyway,' he said, feeling sick.

'Sometimes you are such a ratfink jackass,' she told him, throwing his hand down, some of the shimmery dust on her own fingers.

'Ratfink jackass?' he said. He saw her smirk a little then they both laughed.

She lay down on the damp ground. 'Let's look at clouds,' she said.

Gog lay down next to her so that their shoulders brushed together. They always looked at clouds. Gog tried to send messages to Sunshine through the pictures he saw and imagined she was doing the same; he thought everything anyone said to him had an encoded message, but most were hard to chip away at.

'I can see a heart,' he said.

'That's not a heart,' she told him. 'It's a duck, see?'

He told her that it was definitely a huge heart, then he tilted gradually on to his side so that his face was close to the back of Sunshine's neck. He could see lots of pale, wispy hair on it. He didn't know girls had hair like that on their necks. 'Your breath feels funny,' Sunshine said. 'Like a ghost.'

'Maybe I am a ghost.'

'You're no ghost,' she told him.

He concentrated really hard on his phantom right arm, then he slipped it under Sunshine's shoulders and held her carefully. She felt very fragile, very narrow. Her warm weight pressed on to his arm and he could feel a damp smudge under her armpit. He didn't want to move or breathe. Sunshine turned her head round to look at him, then she rested it back down on the grass and closed her eyes. Neither of them moved. A seagull glided over. The clouds stretched and broke and merged into each other like waves hurrying towards the beach.

'I miss the summer,' Sunshine said. She sounded sleepy.

'It is the summer,' Gog said.

'But I miss it.'

'Yeah,' Gog said. 'We should have done some stuff.'

'I suppose we should have.' She opened her eyes. 'When I look back on it now, I suppose we should have done lots of things.' She sighed and Gog held her more tightly. He cradled and cradled her without her knowing anything about it. Then he moved his phantom hand up and stroked the top of her arm. Her shoulder was thin and bony. He stroked her shoulder with his huge thumb. 'Maybe something will happen, though, before school starts,' she said.

'Like what?' he asked.

'I don't know.' She turned over to face him. He could see dry cracks in her lips. He had to go cross-eyed to look at them because she was so close. She ran her tongue over them. They looked sore.

'You should use Vaseline on your lips,' he said. 'Else they'll split.'

'What? No they won't.'

'They might.'

'I don't need to use any of that crap,' she said. She rolled over and stood up, leaving Gog's phantom arm sprawled out on the ground. She walked away and kicked at some finger bones. In the first week of the holidays they'd been addicted to playing pick-up-sticks with them and the remains of their last game were still there.

It looked like it was going to rain again. Gog thought that he'd better start walking into town but he couldn't leave now because Sunshine was annoyed at him. He knew better than to leave when someone was still annoyed. He hoped his mum had an umbrella with her.

Everything was quiet except for the clacking of bones against bones. He propped himself up on his arm and watched Sunshine. Maybe he should ask her if she wanted to go and take a look at the ribcage. The ribcage was Sunshine's favourite thing in the whole boneyard but Gog hated it. It creeped him out. He didn't know why she liked it so much.

'Hey, did you watch that programme about America last night?' he asked instead.

Sunshine's new plan was to move out there as soon as possible and work in marketing or PR. She stopped kicking and looked around. 'Yeah. It was only OK.'

'When you move out there you'll have to get health insurance. You can't get healthcare free like here.'

'Why not?' she asked. 'What if I can't afford it and I die?'

Gog shrugged. 'I dunno. Everything's different out there.'

'I know. Everyone looks like a movie star. Don't you think that everyone out there looks like a movie star?'

'Maybe not everyone.'

'I'm probably not even going now. The presenter looked like a movie star, didn't she?' She slumped down on to the grass and started picking at it.

'I thought she looked like that man from the chip shop. They have the same nose.'

'Really? Do they?'

He nodded and she grinned up at him. He kept nodding and then he launched into a stuck-in-a-box mime. He didn't have it exactly right yet but that didn't matter. He pushed his hands flat against an invisible barrier over his head. His phantom body stuck out of it at all sides but he tried to ignore it. Sunshine watched him and clapped, but she didn't clap like she meant it. She clapped like she thought it was what she was supposed to do. He dropped his arms.

'We should do something,' Sunshine said. She snapped off a few blades of grass. 'We never do anything.'

Gog looked at his watch. He was definitely late now and his mum didn't like being left on her own. 'I've got to go in a minute.'

She looked up quickly. 'What for?'

'I'm sort of meant to meet Mum in town.'

'Oh. Well in that case I guess you'd better run along.' She yanked up a whole dandelion plant, roots and everything.

'I thought we could go and see the ribcage first,' he said.

She stared up at him, deciding, then nodded and jumped up.

The ribcage was set back from the other bones. It was the only ribcage in the entire place. There should have been more. Gog had found some snapped ribs in among a pile of other bones but that was it. He didn't get that ribcage at all. It was so big, for one thing, way bigger proportionally than any other bone in the yard. It also looked about a million years older. It was gnarled and knotted and stained with yellow and grey. Unlike the other bones, the ribcage had thick clumps of lichen creeping all over it so that it looked half-alive and teeming with furry stars. That's what Gog hated about it. It should be the deadest thing there, deader than anything else, but instead it looked like it was trying to grow back its own skin. He never touched it, but he couldn't take his eyes off it either. Whenever he stood next to it, he felt as if the whole world had been eclipsed by that huge, immobile weave of bones.

Sunshine paced around the ribcage. It towered above her head. She dragged her hand across the ribs as she moved so that her arm dipped between the gaps and slapped against the bones. Each rib was as wide as her handspan.

'Why do you like this thing so much, anyway?' he asked. He stood back and folded his arms.

'Imagine the size of the lungs that would go in here. They'd be so gross. The grossest lungs.'

'Yeah,' he said. He'd never thought of it like that before. Imagine those lungs! Two massive, heaving slabs made up of mottled purple and white and red. They would look like slippery beds. They would loll around like skinned whales on a beach. And yet, what about the power of them? What about the weight and strength that would go behind each breath – the sheer, greedy volumes of air that would circulate and bubble in them? Gog could barely imagine the pressure of all that oxygen, all that life they would trap inside.

'Hey, what's this blue stuff?' Sunshine asked. She was round the other side of the ribcage.

Gog started, thinking about huge distances covered in one stride, how easy it would be to leave everything behind. He walked over to her.

She was laughing. 'Gog, look at this!' There were criss-crossed lines of graffiti sprayed over the bones. The paint was fresh: Gog could smell the chemicals tanging the air. The graffiti looked like it was meant to say something but the bones were too far apart for the word to be legible. Sunshine was laughing about it and asking him what he thought it said. She guessed 'boner'. Gog didn't answer. He touched the paint and traced the marks with his fingers. He couldn't believe someone had done it. He spat on his hand and tried to rub it off. The paint stained his palm turquoise but it stayed on the bones. Sunshine watched but didn't help. Gog rubbed and rubbed at the paint. His heart was thumping hard in his chest. Shreds of blue lichen broke off and crumbled like dry skin.

'Why are you doing that?' Sunshine asked.

He shrugged and stopped. None of the paint had come off. She was looking at him in a strange way. She wanted him to laugh about it, make some joke, say he thought it said 'dick'. Then she would say, 'Maybe *this* is your dad, then.' And even though that's what he had said to her countless times, that his dad was a dick, he would hate her a little bit for saying it back. But he couldn't laugh about it anyway, and that strange tightness between them grew so that something needed to snap. 'Let's get out of here,' she said. 'I'm bored. Let's go to the fountain.'

'The fountain?' Gog said slowly.

'Why are you being weird? You're being really weird. Let's go to the fountain.' She turned to leave.

'What will we do?'

'I don't know. There'll be something good to do there, though,' she said.

'There might not be,' he said. 'There might not be, though.' The gaps between each rib were as broad as Gog's body. He wondered what it would be like to walk in between them. 'How much do you bet me to get inside this?' he said. He turned round but Sunshine was walking away towards the track that led into town. He watched her for a few moments then leaned his head and shoulders into one of the gaps and stepped in. It was like stepping into a cathedral. The ribcage seemed to cut off all sound from outside it. All he could hear was his own breathing. The air it encased seemed thinner and dryer, full of trapped whispers. His mouth went dry. He lay down along the gap where the backbone would have been. The domed roof striped the sky with bones.

Sunshine would almost be in town by now. He could see her walking along: she would be humming; maybe she would hold out her arms and run down the last slope. She might even do a one-handed cartwheel, which she wouldn't do in front of him any more. There was something else he should have said to her but it didn't matter; she'd be outside his house again in the morning. The whole moor was still and the clouds were still. His mum would have given up waiting for him by now. He sighed, and he thought he heard the bones sigh too. He'd go back in a minute; he just wanted to lie in there a bit longer. The ribcage dwarfed him so completely that he couldn't even feel his phantom body any more. He breathed in and out very deeply and, as he did so, he could almost feel the ribcage moving – expanding and contracting with each heave of his chest.

# Beachcombing

*Within easy memory every boat always set aside
a portion of the catch, and left it in a collected heap
on the beach to propitiate the Buccas.*

– Traditions and Hearthside Stories of West Cornwall

## A Knife and Fork

THE THING WAS, did Grandma have any teeth left? Oscar hadn't thought about it before. He had never paid much attention to what she ate or anything like that. He touched the rusty knife and fork they had found at the tideline. They were very heavy and beautiful. One of the fork's prongs was bent inwards, a bit like Oscar's own bottom tooth. He looked up at Grandma, who was sitting next to him on a blue camping chair. 'What do you eat?' he asked her. She was sewing up the part of her mattress where all the stuffing was falling out.

'This and that,' she said. She had the needle in her mouth with the thread trailing out. 'Fish and fat' is what it sounded like. But Grandma definitely didn't eat fish any more – everyone knew that. She didn't even like to talk about it. 'And sometimes that ridiculous lady comes round with meals.' That was where she got all those plastic pots that caught the drips around her bed. With the needle pursed in her mouth like that, it looked like Grandma didn't have any teeth.

But when she took it out, he remembered that she did have all of them, just like everyone else, although hers were browner than his own. It was because she used to clean her teeth with a toothpick and eat Marmite straight out of the jar and drink nothing but strong coffee. She wasn't meant to drink so much coffee any more, but she did, which he wasn't allowed to tell anyone.

'Your teeth are all brown,' he told her. The knife and fork had raised patterns on them. Grandma had given him a bit of sandpaper and he'd managed to rub away most of the rust and dirt. The metal underneath was a dark, silvery colour and there were leaves and swirls. He wanted to eat dinner with them but Grandma said no. 'Who lost these?' he asked suddenly. His bare toes, hanging over the chair, just grazed the cold, damp sand. 'Someone must have lost them.'

'People are careless,' Grandma said. 'Anyone could have lost them.'

'Sometimes it's an accident, though,' Oscar said. He had lost his favourite saucepan because he'd left it on the bus, so he was very sympathetic about other people's losses. 'It's an accident sometimes. It was probably a picnic and then a shipwreck. And everything sank right to the bottom except these.' Grandma nodded but didn't say anything. Her hands fiddled with the thread but didn't do anything with it. She was good at fixing things and didn't even feel the cold. You could tell she didn't feel the cold because of the fact that she lived outside all the time, on the beach. She was very old and old people did die, Oscar knew, and some that were younger, but he didn't think Grandma had even been ill before and usually you were ill before you died, although sometimes it was sudden. The knife and fork felt very heavy. 'I think they're made of silver,' he said. Grandma broke some thread with her teeth. She was strong. She could crush a whole apple in her fist. Oscar got out of the chair and crouched down to poke at some shells and pebbles with his fork. The beach was empty and quiet. It was a long, pale stretch of sand, with high cliffs behind it that curved inwards like the bit of the spoon you ate with, and they sheltered quieter, crescent moons of sand like this one, where Grandma lived. Dark drifts of bladderwrack had heaped up at the tideline and were drying in the air and the wind.

Grandma watched Oscar while she stitched. He looked like a little owl crouched over like that, with his feathery hair tufting up behind his ears. His ears stuck out like his mother's, which was a pity. She could tell he was cold but he didn't like to admit it.

'I think I'll get a jumper on,' she said. He turned round and followed her into the cave, where she kept all her things. He had a spare set of everything there because he visited so often.

'Well, if you are, I suppose I might as well,' he said. He was still clutching the knife and fork, and they poked through a loose part of the wool so that one arm got trapped and Grandma had to get it out. 'What about that cow that fell on the beach?' he said. 'Did you see it?'

'I told you I didn't see it.'

'Who did see?'

'I don't know. All the people on the beach, I suppose.' Last summer, a cow had fallen off the cliff and on to the beach and Oscar wished that he had seen it. He didn't know anyone who had. He looked at his knife and fork. He didn't let go of them all afternoon, then later, before he went home, he laid them carefully down in the corner next to his other precious things.


## Bucca Trails

Grandma showed him how to spot bucca trails. It was important information to know. Buccas had been during the night, Grandma said, although it was calm now and still. It was mid-morning and the tide was right out. There were bucca trails everywhere. 'Did you hear them, in the night?' Oscar asked. Grandma nodded. In fact, they had poked their heads right inside the cave to take a look at her. Now that they had gone, you could see exactly where they'd come from and which direction they had left in. The sand was covered in the wide, arcing imprints of their movements. It looked like someone had swept a huge broom in a curve from the sea up to the cliffs and then back again, or someone had rushed across the sand wearing a long, heavy skirt.

Grandma showed him how the disturbed sand was sitting loosely on top, waiting to be packed back in. She bent down slowly and poked at it and said a few things to herself. 'South-westerly,' she said. 'Force four.' Oscar nodded. He knew about south-westerly and force four. Grandma straightened up and then stared out at the sea. She was very still. Oscar found a stick and started to draw a pattern. Grandma stared out to sea. Her back was very straight and aching down at the bottom.

'Why can't we ever see them?' Oscar asked. This is what he knew about buccas: you can't actually see them; you can only see what they do to other things. So, if the sand is whirling around and the waves are white and choppy and your hair is whipped up and around then there is probably a bucca. And if the rain is pushed one way or the other, like curtains. And they like to eat fish, and if you leave a fish on the beach the buccas will leave your boats alone, but if you don't they get very angry. And sometimes you can hear them, especially when there are hundreds of them rushing in off the sea so that their bodies brush against the waves and the sand and the air rushes through their open mouths. But still, he wasn't exactly sure why you couldn't see them. This is what he wanted to know: were they invisible?

'Not invisible,' Grandma said.

'But how come we can't see them, then?'

'They don't have bodies like us. You have to see them in other ways.' Grandma looked down at Oscar, who had started to scratch around with his stick again. 'We talked about that before.'

He shrugged and carried on scratching. He was hungry. They sounded invisible to him. And if they weren't invisible, how come that thing about Grandpa and Uncle Jack?

'It's important to be able to see the signs,' Grandma carried on. She coughed a few times, loudly and hard and with a wheeze at the end. She really did need to teach him all the signs. She started to explain about the direction of the tracks and what they meant, and if the sea is very calm but there's a sickly green light then you have to be particularly careful. Oscar was humming to himself. 'You're not even listening, are you?' Grandma said.

Oscar jumped up. 'You're not listening to me!' he said. 'It's you who isn't listening to me.' He ran crazily around her legs, flinging sand on to his jeans.

Grandma didn't watch him running. 'You can go if you want,' she said. He was boring when he was like this. Oscar stopped running and leaned against her legs. He wouldn't go yet. They ought to follow the trails right down to the tideline and see what happened. But first, Grandma had to cough some more, and she rubbed the bottom of her back and bent her back down and coughed so hard it sounded like she was going to be sick. Then she spat something out.

'Gross,' Oscar said.

'Don't be wet,' Grandma told him. She covered the thing over with sand and they followed a line of shells and seaweed and sticks that the buccas had bowled along the beach. Oscar kept stopping and poking, stopping and poking, and Grandma waited for him. The beach leading up to the tideline was covered in purple and grey pebbles, and as the sea pulled back from them, it sounded like a million people were popping bubble wrap all at once. There was sea foam floating at the edge and it looked like bits of old omelette. Oscar thought about throwing some at Grandma but decided not to. She hadn't liked it before and then she had thrown some back and it smelled like drains.

The buccas had gone away now, but they would be back. They lingered right out at sea and waited. Grandma knew everything about them. She sniffed the air and knew when they'd come back. She was wearing one of Grandpa's big jumpers. It was dark blue and probably had never been washed because it was salty and stiff when you touched the wool, and smelled of two hundred things, including smoke. He touched the fraying sleeve.

'This was his favourite,' Grandma said. 'He used to wear it whenever . . .'

And the smoke was like the smoke from frying sausages. 'What's for lunch?' Oscar asked. It wasn't time yet but he was so hungry. Grandma sighed and rubbed her back once more. Then they turned round and started walking home.

## Three Feathers and a Pair of Glasses

Grandma's cough got worse so she couldn't go out on to the beach. She had to stay in her chair at the mouth of the cave with a blanket over her knees. Sometimes she kicked it off and stamped on it and said 'damn thing', but she always put it back on again. Oscar had brought it with him the day before with the milk, plus some medicine and instructions to tell Grandma that she would die if she didn't stop being a stubborn fool and move off the beach. It was all from Oscar's parents, who, although they refused to visit Grandma and hadn't spoken to her properly for years, still kept her room ready in the house for when she wanted to come back.

'The doctor says I'm fine. As strong as a horse,' Grandma said. 'A cough could happen to anyone.' They were eating clementines. It was early spring and still chilly. Grandma had to pick off all the pith before she could eat a segment. It took her a long time. Oscar ate his, pith and all, and Grandma couldn't watch. After a while, Oscar wandered off a little way to investigate a heap of bits and pieces that he had seen. The water was choppy today and the gulls were restless – bickering and not settling down. They would land on a rock and then take off again straight away. They were getting bigger. Grandma was sure they were getting bigger. They interfered with her concentration. Everything seemed damp today as well, and cold, and sounds had an almost-echo. She felt like she was in a church; she felt like she was constantly in a church. She had thought that winter was over, but here it was lingering like sea mist over the beach. It had been an especially hard winter this year and she was trying not to think about the next one.

She watched Oscar further down the beach. He was stamped darkly on to the wide stretch of sea like a single footprint. After a while he came back up holding a handful of things. 'It has been a very good day for finding things,' he said solemnly. 'One of the best, probably.'

'Don't rub it in,' Grandma told him. 'What have you got?' Oscar put everything down then picked out his first item. It was a feather. He gave it to Grandma, who inspected it and nodded, confirming that it was a good one. 'Black-backed gull,' she said. 'Good condi-tion.' The feather was shiny and dark with a white tip at the end. It was big, too, bigger than Grandma's hand-span and she had big hands; maybe it was as long as her feet. She handed it back and Oscar gave her the next thing. It was another feather. This one was smaller and a purer black. It was slightly raggedy and threadbare – the edges were askew and worn. 'Chough,' Grandma said. 'These are rare. There are only two nesting pairs. Pity it's not in better nick.' Oscar took it back and tried to smooth everything the right way. He wanted to know whether it hurt birds when their feathers fell out. Grandma said it didn't. It was just like when Oscar's hair fell out – he probably didn't even notice it.

'My hair doesn't fall out!' he said. 'Look.' He pointed at his head to show there weren't any gaps. Grandma snorted but didn't say anything else. Oscar looked at her warily and rubbed over his hair a few times, checking his palms afterwards.

'What else is there?' Grandma asked. There was one more feather, which was Oscar's favourite. It was white and small and quite fluffy around the edges. Grandma looked at it for a long time. There was a pale grey streak veining through it. She didn't actually know what this feather was. She recognised it, but she couldn't think of the name. She used to know the name. She stroked it and stroked it and struggled to think of the name but she couldn't. 'Juvenile guillemot,' she said, which was all she could think of.

Oscar nodded and took it back. 'Guillemot,' he said to himself. 'Guillemot.'

Grandma coughed a bit and cleared her throat. 'Is that every-thing?' she said. Oscar shook his head and then picked up something else. It was an old pair of glasses. They didn't have any lenses in them and the frames were thin and black. The right arm was bent outwards and the left arm was bent inwards. It was an excellent find. Oscar put them on and they slid down to the end of his nose. He wouldn't let anyone else try them on.

Grandma felt drawn to the glasses although she didn't know why. There was something morbid about them because they were probably a dead person's glasses, but she did very much want to try them on. 'Can I try them on, Oscar?' she asked. Oscar pretended that he hadn't heard. Grandma decided to bide her time. After a while she suggested a game of blackjack. She had taught Oscar how to play a year ago so she could win his pocket money off him.

'OK,' he said. He got the cards and another chair and the board that they balanced on their knees as a table. Grandma dealt two cards each. Oscar studied his cards. He studied the coins Grandma had next to her. Then he laid down the gull feather. He asked for another card and frowned when he got it. He counted on his fingers then asked for another. He got an eight, so Grandma got the feather. At the next deal he beat Grandma and won two pounds. He lost both feathers after that but he'd counted wrong so it was a let. But he lost them again straight after. Grandma dealt again and Oscar grinned. He had good cards. He put the glasses down on the table. He was confident. 'Hit me,' he said. Grandma turned a card over. It was a three. 'Hit me,' he said again. It was a seven. 'Hit me,' he said. It was another seven. 'Arse cheeks,' he said and threw his cards down. Grandma raised her eyebrow at him. He scowled and pushed over the glasses. 'They don't even work, anyway.' She put the glasses on and wore them for the rest of the afternoon. They fitted her quite well, although the arm dug in behind her ear and after a while it got annoying so she took them off. She would play Oscar again later and let him win them back.

## *Fish Bones*

When Oscar found the fish bones, he put them straight into his pocket and didn't tell Grandma. They had been walking over the other side of the beach and Grandma had gone behind a rock to do some private business. At first he thought they were smooth white stones, sea-battered stones, but then he saw that they looked very much like a head and a spine. On closer inspection, this was exactly what they were, and there was a small fin that looked like a fragile comb. The skull still had the jaw intact and had holes for eyes. The spine was longer than his middle finger and had spikes and ridges down it. He looked around for Grandma but couldn't see her. Then he picked up the three bones and put them in the pocket of his school trousers.

Grandma saw him bend over and then put something in his pocket. She thought he must have found something really good, but when she went over he didn't tell her about it. He probably wanted to keep it all to himself, the greedy little git. 'Find anything?' she asked.

'Nope,' he said. He put his hands in his pockets and shrugged his shoulders. He had his lying face on – one eyebrow raised up and twitching a bit, and his nostrils flaring. He'd show her what it was later; he wouldn't be able to resist.

It was getting warmer. The thrift was coming out along the cliffs, and the campion and the mesembryanthemum. There were more people turning up now, walking or sometimes flying a kite. The buccas came in sporadic waves: one moment they were gone, the next they gusted in like a slap and set your clothes and hair and the sand flying. You had to be careful at this time of year – they always came when they weren't expected. In fact, it was likely that they'd be coming any time now. The sky was getting darker and clouds which hadn't been there before were crowding in like faces. 'It's going to rain,' she said.

'Is it?' Oscar asked. 'How do you know?'

'I can smell it,' Grandma said.

Oscar sniffed. 'I can smell it too,' he said.

'What can you smell?' Grandma asked.

Oscar sniffed again. He could definitely smell it. 'I can smell . . . It smells like . . .' He stopped walking and kicked at a stone while he thought. 'Like the sky is damp paper,' he said at last. Grandma nodded and agreed and asked him to hurry up if they didn't want to get drenched: she could see buccas' footprints on the sea. They didn't make it in time. The rain started and it was the kind of rain that soaked through your clothes in seconds. It was the kind of rain Grandma called a bastard rain and shook her fist at once they were back in the cave, even though she knew it was their own fault because they hadn't been paying enough attention.

They had to get changed into dry clothes. Oscar took the fish bones out of his pocket and hid them underneath his schoolbag. Grandma saw him hide something but didn't mention it. She got changed and then Oscar got changed, but he fidgeted and wanted Grandma to turn around the other way while he did it, which was new. So Grandma listened to him getting changed and watched a dark vein of water slide down the wall. When he was done, she put some water in the kettle and lit the camping stove.

'Looks like we won't get out again today,' she said.

It seemed colder inside the cave and Oscar wanted to go home but he was staying for dinner. 'It might stop,' he said, but Grandma shook her head and she knew these things because she and Grandpa and Uncle Jack had all been fishermen and fishermen knew everything about outside and the weather. There was always a drip drip drip inside the cave that Grandma caught in the plastic pots. She had two wind-up lamps, a stove, a fold-out table and camping chairs. There was her mattress, too, and leather suitcases that she kept clothes in. On one wall there was a row of Chinese painted plates and in one corner there was a rock painted like an orange cat.

Grandma made coffee for them both. She was trying to wean Oscar on to it. Everyone liked good strong coffee, she said, it was good for you. But she did add a lot of milk to his and half a teaspoon of sugar. Then she got out the box of bourbons and they both pulled the top of the biscuit off and scraped the buttercream with their teeth. The rain didn't make much sound as it hit the sand outside. Sometimes, a bucca would throw a handful of rain right into the cave, and it would drill shallow holes into the sand around the entrance.

Oscar and Grandma both got bored quickly. It was hours until dinner. Grandma wanted to read, but Oscar's scuffing and sighing would have put her off. Oscar wanted to play with the fish bones but he couldn't while Grandma was there. He started piling up stones in tottering columns and then when they fell down both he and Grandma jumped. Then he scratched at the wall with a pencil until the lead snapped.

'For God's sake!' Grandma said. 'Why don't you just get out whatever it is you've hidden under there and play with that?'

'Hidden?' Oscar said.

'You know what I'm talking about,' Grandma said. 'You can't stop looking at where you put it. Stop hoarding it away like a miser.'

'What's a miser?' he asked.

'A skinflint,' Grandma said.

'There isn't anything,' Oscar said.

'Fine,' Grandma said and crossed her arms. They sat in silence for a while, listening to the drips and the buccas, and to each other breathing. Grandma got out her book and pretended to read. After a while she asked Oscar if he would mind poking his head out to see exactly what the weather was doing. Then, once he was over at the front of the cave, she went over and picked up his schoolbag to see what was underneath. She was still holding the bag and staring at the fish bones when Oscar turned round to tell her about the weather.

'You cheat!' he yelled, hurrying over. 'That's a cheat.' Grandma didn't say anything. She just kept looking at the fish bones bedded down in the grey sand. She hardly heard anything that Oscar was saying. As soon as she saw those bones she was up and away and back in her old kitchen with the smell of the soup she was cooking, and the tang of resin from the table she'd been sanding, and that trickle of condensed steam running down the window and on to the draining board with a hollow tap. Tap. Tap. As she opened the window to let some air in, she noticed how quickly the wind was getting up. The washing was billowing out like swans lumbering out of water. It was billowing out and snapping backwards and the lime trees were shivering. At that moment she realised that she had forgotten, for the first time ever, to put a fish out on the sand for the buccas before her husband and her son went out for the morning catch. There was nothing to do except watch the buccas lurch into a storm and wait.

Tap. Tap. The window slammed shut. The next day she had moved out on to the beach and she hadn't been back into a house since. And now Oscar had brought fish bones into the cave! He might as well be poking her eyes out with them.

'Grandma?' Oscar asked. Her eyes looked all funny, and her mouth. She wasn't meant to have seen those bones. No one talked to Grandma about fish and now she'd seen his fish bones. 'Grandma?' he asked again. 'You shouldn't have looked at my hiding place.' He stared at her some more. 'Should you?' Grandma backed down on to the floor and folded her arms around herself. Her arms and hands looked frail and bony – but she could crush a whole apple in her fist! Oscar sat down next to her and folded his arms around himself. 'Should you?' he asked again. After a while, he started to stroke and pat the top of Grandma's arm with his fingers. Grandma's arm was still and stiff. She could see the washing billowing out and then snapping backwards. Then she shook her head and coughed and it was like she was waking up. She put her hand on the top of his head and mussed the hair all around, roughly and gently all at the same time, so that it stuck up like the brush she used to sweep the sand away from her bed.

## A Door

The important thing to remember when Mr Rogers came over to argue with Grandma was to stay out the way of his stick because he whirled it around a lot when he thought the conversation was flagging. Grandma said that when he tapped Oscar with it, it was out of respect, but Oscar knew better. He and Mr Rogers had a silent, secret battle going on. Neither of them knew why it had started, but they knew it wasn't going to end.

This was what happened whenever he came to see Grandma: the first anyone knew of it was when he limped up the beach like a bedraggled seagull, wheezing loudly and thumping hard on his chest. As soon as that happened, Grandma hurried to fold out the extra chair and get out the box of marshmallows to put on the table. Mr Rogers ate a lot of marshmallows because he said they kept him glued together on the inside. Oscar told Grandma that it was stupid of Mr Rogers to think that and Grandma said, 'Everyone has their excuses.'

It was vital to have everything out and ready and then to sit around and pretend that you always knew Mr Rogers was coming and were waiting for him to arrive all this time. If things were brought out especially for him while he was there he got nervous and thumped his chest and didn't talk much, and if you hadn't prepared anything at all he might just carry on straight past and not talk to you for a long time after. Then, while he sat down, you had to carry on talking and not really notice him until he was comfortable and ready to start talking himself. It all had to be done exactly right, which is just what you have to do with some people.

It was the worst of all possible times for him to have come. Oscar had found an entire door on the other side of the beach and was going to surprise Grandma with it after lunch. It was probably the best thing he'd ever found. It was a whole door just lying there on a carpet of grey stones. It was painted white and there was a letterbox and it hardly had any dents or chips in it. He hadn't even opened the door because he thought Grandma might want to do it, and also because of the angle he probably wouldn't be able to on his own anyway. But now Mr Rogers had come and he didn't deserve to see the door – it was too good a thing. So the tide would take it and they wouldn't get to see it again.

Mr Rogers dragged himself up the beach towards them. Apparently he might have seen the cow fall on to the beach but Oscar had never asked him about it. Oscar bent down, picked up handfuls of sand and rubbed them into his shoes. He lifted himself up off the chair with both hands on the plastic arms and swung his legs forwards. He kicked Grandma's knees by accident and she said 'Jesus Christ' and scowled at him, so he slunk right down and picked at his lips. The tide was going to turn soon and take away the door.

Anyway, maybe Grandma didn't deserve the door today? She seemed angry and annoyed and she wasn't talking very much. She had forgotten to go and get the box of marshmallows, so he'd had to do it himself, and he'd had to fold out the extra chair. He usually left as soon as Mr Rogers had sat down and started talking, but perhaps he ought to stay for a while and make sure Grandma was all right.

Grandma wanted Oscar to go away. She felt tired today – too tired to faff about entertaining, but there was nothing to be done about it. Her problem was that she would have to sit and argue with Mr Rogers. He always wanted to have a heated debate which ended up with them saying things like 'you jackass' to each other, whether she wanted to or not.

Mr Rogers sat down and he smelled of petrol and Vosene. His throat sounded like it was as narrow as a piece of thread and he cracked his knuckles and scratched deep inside his ears so that it looked like his finger should get stuck in there. He had two toes missing and had never even shown Oscar. Grandma called him an old acquaintance, whatever that was. While Mr Rogers was getting settled, Grandma stared at him instead of ignoring him. She was doing it all wrong, so Oscar had to show her a scab on his leg to distract her until Mr Rogers was ready to talk. It wasn't even a very good scab and Grandma probably thought he was showing off about it, which he wasn't.

'The boy hasn't grown,' Mr Rogers eventually said to Grandma.

'He's sitting down,' Grandma said. 'It's hard for you to tell.'

'Where's his purse?' Oscar had carried a purse around for a while and Mr Rogers hadn't seemed to like it.

'He's moved on,' Grandma said.

Oscar swung his legs and thought about the door. He imagined the tide creeping in like fingers and his chest was tight and fluttery.

Something wasn't right with the argument that Mr Rogers and Grandma were having. They always argued about the same kinds of things, and they said the same things each time and then they said, 'It was good to have got that off my chest.' They argued about boring things like the weather changing, or old films, or about people they used to know. But today Grandma wasn't sticking to her side of the argument; it was almost as if she was about to agree with Mr Rogers, and Mr Rogers was looking nervous and clearing his throat and thumping his chest.

'They're just fiddling the stats, fiddling the stats is all they're doing,' Mr Rogers said.

'Perhaps they are, yes,' Grandma said. She looked tired and distracted and couldn't seem to remember what part of the argument to take. She should be saying something else now; she should be saying something about how paranoid Mr Rogers was. Oscar stared at her. Mr Rogers had angled his chair away from him on purpose, which he always did. Oscar wanted to go away and see the door by himself and leave them to it, but there was a horrible silence that went on and on and on and so, before he really knew what he was doing, he said, 'I have to show you both something before the tide gets it. It's very important.'

He took them to the door. It was just as beautiful as it had been earlier. He looked at Grandma anxiously to make sure she liked it. He didn't want it to be a waste. She was examining it carefully. 'If we opened it,' Oscar said, 'where would it go?'

Mr Rogers snorted. 'To the stones underneath, I reckon,' he said. He didn't deserve the door and he was ruining it, just like Oscar knew he would. He was tapping at it with his stick and some of the paint was chipping off.

'Under the sea?' Grandma asked. Oscar shrugged.

'Maybe,' he said. 'But maybe it would go back into the room it came off, and you could walk in and be inside the room.' He only looked at Grandma when he said that. Grandma nodded and said that was a better idea than hers because hers was obvious.

'Let's open it and see, shall we?' Mr Rogers asked. He poked at the letterbox with the stick. Oscar's heart dropped. He didn't want to. It was his door. He shouldn't have let anyone else see it. He would have to open it now and Mr Rogers would be right because it wouldn't really go anywhere. He walked around the door, figuring out where he should stand to open it.

'We can't open it,' Grandma said.

'Why?' Mr Rogers asked.

'It wouldn't be the done thing,' Grandma said. 'Would it, Oscar?'

Oscar stopped walking, shook his head and glared at Mr Rogers. 'It wouldn't be the done thing,' he said.

The water was just starting to reach the door. Grandma watched Oscar as he walked ahead with his hands in his pockets. It had been a very generous gesture, him taking them to the door, she knew. She caught up with him. 'It was one of the best doors I've seen,' she whispered as they walked back.

'I know,' Oscar said.

## The Whale

It was going to be a summer of storms and no doubt about it. Grandma could feel it in the air as soon as she woke up. There had been a spate of storms for the last few days and they were going to carry on. They were the sort of storms that came all at once, loudly and hurriedly and brashly, and then burnt themselves out quickly. She went to the mouth of the cave and looked out. The sea looked swollen and dark grey. It was ugly a lot of the time, the sea, if you really looked at it. Ugly and beautiful too, with its muscles and its shadows and its deep mutterings, as if it was constantly arguing with itself. Sometimes she hated it and sometimes she loved it, which was the same with anything, she supposed. Once, a storm had blown in hundreds, thousands, of pieces of foam. The white foam had raced in like a flock of birds and each piece glided down and landed on the beach or on the cliff grass like sandpipers landing. Sometimes she wondered whether all she was doing here was waiting for that to happen again. Storms were because of the buccas. They did beautiful as well as terrible things; she could see that. She had to keep an eye on them. That was all she could do.

She needed things for the cave. She needed batteries and milk and camping gas. Oscar was meant to be bringing them this morning; he'd better not have forgotten. Still, it was early yet. She was always up early. If you weren't up before seven you might as well not get up at all. The first thing to do when she got up was heat some water in a saucepan for a wash. She had saved just enough gas for that. Then she washed behind her woven screen, one half at a time so she didn't get too cold. Then layers: tights, trousers, socks, vest, several tops and a jumper. Then she put the water on for coffee and spooned in the coffee and the secret teaspoon of sugar she had now when no one else was around. And in her head she could see the window in her old kitchen slamming shut, and the washing stretching and billowing out and snapping back on the line. She sipped her coffee. And eventually, as it always did now, the movement of the washing turned into a song, or a tune she thought she'd forgotten, and she swept the sand away from the bed, humming it.

Everything seemed to need fixing suddenly. The mattress was splitting again and the wind-up light kept blinking. She would need a better sleeping bag for next winter. Maybe she could send Oscar into the shop to look at them for her. But his mother was bound to find out and she didn't want her to know about the sleeping bag. Anyway, it was summer first. Summer first, so that didn't matter.

Where was Oscar? He ought to be here by now with her things so that he wouldn't be late for school. She sat on the bed and waited, then went out on to the beach. There was someone walking but it wasn't Oscar. She really did need those batteries. And she was going to tell him about what the buccas had sounded like in the storm last night, how they'd sounded like migrating ghosts.

She started to walk up the beach, following the figure she had seen hurrying past. The figure joined a group of people up ahead and suddenly there was a huge whale lying on the beach like a shipwreck and the people were gathered around it as if it was a campfire.

Grandma went a bit closer but she stayed near the rocks that jutted out from the cliff. It was a fin whale, at least fifty feet long, which must have been washed ashore during the night. It was pale, almost sand-coloured, but there were also darker marks that criss-crossed one another close to the tail. The tail itself was so big, so powerful-looking, that it was hard to imagine there wasn't any life left in it.

Oscar was there, standing next to his mother, wide-eyed and rigid, staring up at the whale with amazement and horror and wonder. The sides of the whale were taller than his head. He looked at it, then at the sea, then back at the whale as if he had never quite believed that such things existed in there, as if the whale had made the depths and the shifts and the floors of the sea suddenly clear to him.

Grandma kept close to the rocks. Oscar had forgotten her for now – he wouldn't be coming over today. She didn't blame him.

Oscar's mother looked at her watch and then leaned down and said something to him. They took one last look at the whale and then started to walk quickly along the beach, ready to cut up one of the dunes to the road to get to school. They would have to pass the spot where Grandma was. She hid. She wasn't exactly sure why. She just saw them coming towards her and she hid. She'd always had a knack for hiding. She crawled under an overarching bit of rock and tucked her knees up as far as they would go and then stayed very still. She couldn't see whether they had gone past or not so she waited there, crouched down, feeling ridiculous, until she was sure they wouldn't see her when she crawled out.


## A Piece of the Moon

It was probably too high to reach. It was right above them, snagged on to the cliff above the cave, next to the thrift's bobbing hats and the

126

stone that looked like a face. It was late in the afternoon when Oscar spotted it. It was a thick, white, bright shape that looked like it had fallen from somewhere very far away. It was all crumpled up but still glowing very slightly like a night light. It could be many things. But the thing was, it was so difficult to tell, and Oscar felt like he really needed to know what it was. Sometimes he didn't really care what things were and sometimes he did. When he looked up at it from one angle it looked like one thing and then from another it looked completely different.

Oscar was staying over for the first time in the year because the nights were just warm enough now. He had brought over his rucksack and his own cereal because he didn't like the stuff Grandma got in. He had an airbed and a sleeping bag and a torch. It was early evening. There was a party going on somewhere along the beach because they could see a bonfire and hear laughing and whoops. The tide was in and the sky was covered in dark blue clouds. The water was dark blue and barely moved.

Oscar paced around the bottom of the cliff, looking up. Grandma told him to relax but he couldn't. What he needed to do was climb up there and see for himself, but it was too high. Almost too high – he might be able to do it or he might not. He decided he couldn't, and went into the cave. Grandma followed him inside and got him peeling carrots for dinner. He couldn't concentrate, though, because he could tell it was still up there and he didn't know what it was. He thought he knew, because of the glow. He wondered if it would be hot or cold to touch. It was going to start getting properly dark in a few hours. Maybe the buccas would steal it in the night and then he would never know. He went back out and paced around the bottom of the rock.

'What are you doing?' Grandma asked.

'Thinking,' Oscar said. He would be a coward if he didn't climb up there. No one would know he had been one except himself. But he would always know, which was his biggest problem.

Grandma looked up and saw the white, glowing thing. 'What is that?' It was so hard to tell – it looked shapeless, but then sometimes it looked like a crumpled triangle, and other times a pale, curving arm. She could see Oscar's problem. It was too high really, but it was too low to abandon altogether. He was going to have to climb up there. 'You're going to have to climb up there,' she said. 'I'll come up as well.'

'You aren't meant to climb,' Oscar said.

'Neither are you.'

Grandma went first. It was easy to start with because the rock went up in a series of wide, flat steps that they could wait on while Grandma coughed and caught her breath. Oscar coughed too, to make her feel better, until Grandma told him to stop faking it. Then they scrambled up a steeper bit and rested on another platform. Oscar kicked some gravel over the edge and it pattered on to the cave's roof. After a while they hoisted themselves up to the next flat platform and sat down. There wasn't anywhere to go next. There was a shelf of rock blocking the way above and nothing to grip on to either side. They could see out over the whole beach from their ledge. There was the party – a whole lot of tiny black shapes floating in front of a fire. You couldn't hear them from up here. You couldn't really hear anything.

'We can't go any further,' Grandma said.

'No,' he replied. After a while he said, 'It doesn't matter.'

'It doesn't matter at all,' Grandma said.

'We might fall off, like that cow.'

Grandma said that they wouldn't.

Oscar said, 'Lisa at school said you must be the most unhappy person in the whole world.'

'Lisa is a shit,' Grandma said. Oscar nodded. She was a shit. 'I am certainly not the unhappiest person in the world.'

'I said that. I said to her that Grandma is certainly not that. I said: Grandma is keeping on, which is very different.'

'Where did you get that from?'

Oscar shrugged. 'I don't know.' They looked out over the beach. It was important to have come this far.

# Notes from the House Spirits

THERE IS A SUDDEN silence and then everything is the same. An empty house is never silent for long and a house is never empty because we are here. There is a sudden silence and then everything is the same. Nothing is ever exactly the same, but it goes back to how it was. The staircase creaks and relaxes, the air slows and stills in rooms.

The buddleia in the attic is growing. We dream, as we have always dreamt, of doors and windows under water, of walls under water. We try not to dwell on these dreams.

Dust drifts across the room and settles on skirting and curtain rails. We can see it, every single piece, as it piles up and no one brushes it away. Dust is static and lazy; it lands on the first thing it sees. It fills the house bit by bit and no one brushes it away. It is not our job to brush it away.

This one left suddenly in the night. She sat up quickly in bed, swung her legs on to the floor and walked down the stairs. She stretched out her arms but there was no one else there. She talked to someone that we couldn't see. 'There you are,' she said. 'You didn't take your boots off. Will I need a coat?' She went out the front door and she left it open.

Things we glimpse out of the front door:
Other rooms.
Other houses.
One huge space like a silent kitchen, with small lights on and one crescent of light, as if someone had left the fridge door open.

It is rude to leave suddenly, without any notice. She didn't give us any notice. There weren't any boxes. She didn't take any of her things away. Didn't she like it here? She left all her things behind. What does she expect us to do with it all? There is nothing that we can do with it, except count it, except look carefully through it, and we have done that already.

We back away, us, the house, towards keyholes and gaps. Now there is the house and there are the other things. We have retreated. They have become left-behind things. They have become awkward and extra, things that don't belong. It is inevitable.

Now we notice what we didn't notice before: that the paint is actually a strange blue, a cold blue, a blue that wasn't the right decision. We don't want that blue any more. We pick at it and bits fall on to the carpet. We notice how thin the carpet is getting. We notice how the clocks make the walls sound hollow. We don't like the walls to sound hollow so we stop the hands on one or two clocks, but only on one or two, and maybe we loosen the battery in the back of another.

*　　*　　*

Sometimes a light shines through the window and it looks as if some-one has turned on a light downstairs. Sometimes a voice calls through the house, we feel some weight on the stairs; or a coat, a dress left hang-ing in a cupboard seems rounder, body-shaped, like there is someone inside it. There is a flash on a door handle as if a hand were reaching out to open it, but there is no hand. We are the only ones left.

Things we miss about the one who left suddenly in the night:
Her laugh, which was as loud and sudden as the gas flame igniting in the boiler.
The kettle's click and whoosh and teaspoons tapping like rain against the windows.
Her television with all its bright colours and its other houses.
The way she jumped when the doorbell rang.
The way we had to make sure the walls caught her when she stumbled.

That smokiness brews up and gets into the curtains. We don't know where it comes from. There is a spider's web behind a door handle and one under a light switch. We like spiders; they are quiet and make good use of the space.

Leaves come in under the door and we pick them up by their stalks and let them out through the letterbox.

Somebody comes and turns off the fridge and the freezer and the boiler. Perhaps we have seen her before. We are not good with faces. For a moment, we think that the woman who left in the night has come back. This new person watches as the freezer shud-ders, then starts to drop pieces of ice. She stands there, watching.

She doesn't do anything except watch as the ice drops and melts on the floor.

Now that there is no noise from the fridge and the freezer and the boiler, we can hear other things. We can hear the pictures beginning to tilt off centre.

The telephone has been left plugged in and sometimes it rings. Sometimes we hear a familiar voice, always saying the same thing: 'I'm not here at the moment. Please leave a message and I'll get back to you.' It is strange, hearing that voice again, and we look around, half expecting to see someone. At least, we think the voice is familiar – we are not good with voices. It is easy for us to forget.

Sometimes we listen to the messages but we do not understand them.

'Hello, I thought I'd ring for a quick catch-up. It's been a long time. Sorry it's been so long. How is everything?'

'The book you ordered is now ready to be picked up.'

'Is this the right number? Do you still live here?'

The shoes are packed into boxes and the boxes are stacked up like bricks. The mirrors are taken down and the walls are just walls again, which is a relief.

There is always somebody who sorts through the left-behind things and turns off the boiler. The woman's footsteps are light and slow. She stares out of the window. She talks on the phone. She puts on one of the jumpers from the wardrobe and wears it all the time, even when she's asleep. It is too small for her. Once, she drops a glass as she is packing, and she looks down at the pieces and then drops the rest, glass by glass, which is probably the clumsiest thing we have ever seen.

She takes the cushions off the sofa and moves it away from the wall. There is something in the empty space. There are small round balls, made out of butter, covered in dust and hair. The woman who left in the night used to cover them in sugar and make anyone who came over eat them. We didn't know that most people dropped them behind the sofa. We didn't know they were there. They are covered in dust and hair. The woman with light, slow footsteps puts her hand over her mouth and stares down at the butterballs. We didn't know they were there. It is not our job to clear things away. They are the only thing we have ever missed.

The house is bare. People come and go, mostly in pairs.

We didn't know those butterballs were there. They are the only thing we have ever missed.

'Would this be our bedroom? I'm not sure if I see this as our bedroom,' they say. They say, 'What do you think?' They look at their reflections in the windows and they look faint and lost. They keep to the edges of the rooms. They sit on the edge of the bath and look down into the plughole. They investigate the pale grey fingerprints on a wall. They lean backwards and measure out invisible objects with their arms.

They are always drawn to the attic. We don't know why.

Things left behind in the attic:
    A rocking horse with a missing eye.
    A plastic skull.

A suitcase stuffed full of receipts and discount vouchers.
A roll of carpet.
A cricket bat and a deflated football.
Four nails and six drawing pins.
A bunch of dry white flowers.

The attic is a strange place. There are gaps and spaces that lead outside. There are silverfish and seeds and pollen and old cooking smells. Buddleia is growing through the wall. There are things that people have hoarded and left behind.

Once, somebody's legs went through the attic floor because they weren't careful. They didn't step in the right places. Just their legs dangling and us wringing our hands and watching. Plaster everywhere. It is our job to protect the house. Why do they always want to go into the attic? We don't know why.

The buddleia shrivels and dries to husks. The cold enters the house and so does someone new. The boiler is switched on and there are boxes. He moves them in himself, without any help. Most of the boxes are left in the second bedroom and they are not unpacked. There are no proper beds. He unrolls a mat and sleeps on it. He stays up late, staring at the television or at the computer. The room flickers blue and green. He goes to the fridge, to the sofa, to the bathroom, and on his way between rooms he knocks into the walls with his shoulders.

We dream, and in our dream there is a sudden rush of water. Doors and windows soak and split. They lift away from their frames and disappear. Lampshades and clocks float past.

*  *  *

Two children come. The man makes them food and puts it on their plates in the shape of a face. He hadn't turned the oven on before they arrived. The boy looks pleased with his food but the girl scowls and picks at the eyes. The table is too small for three people so they keep knocking knees and elbows. 'What do you want to do?' the man asks them. He isn't eating anything. They shrug. 'Is there a cat here? You said you would get a cat.'

'I haven't got a cat yet,' he says.

'You said you would get one,' they tell him. They look around at the bare house.

We have seen cats before. They stare at us and bristle. We don't like them. We have seen children before. They move around so quickly that we can't keep track of which room they are in. These children are different. They don't move quickly; they kick at the edges of things. They don't seem interested in the house. They trail after each other and when they sit, they fall back with all of their weight so that the sofa bumps into the wall.

Now and again, when the children aren't there, a woman comes over to stay. We don't know if we recognise her. We aren't very good with faces. Sometimes, when she goes to the bathroom, she turns up the television first, but we don't know why she would do this. We are probably the only ones who notice. When she can't find her watch, we find it for her, and put it in the pocket of her coat, but then she shouts that she has already looked in the pocket of her coat. We were only trying to help. It is not our job to find things. They step on each other's feet in the kitchen. They move their chairs closer together, slowly, during dinner.

'What are you thinking about?' she asks him, smiling, leaning close.

He looks at his fork. 'The Spanish Revolution,' he says.

'OK,' she says. 'OK.'

They raise their forks and lower them in unison.

Number of tiles on the roof: 874. There were 876 but two disappeared and no one has replaced them.

Leaves come in under the door and we post them out through the letterbox.

Two new ones. They keep close together. There is only ever one light on because they are always in the same room. They don't have any real furniture; they have furniture that doesn't look solid. You can fold it. We have never seen folding furniture. There's no fridge yet, only a gap where the fridge should be. They keep their milk in a saucepan of cold water. We are not sure how well they will look after the house. Nothing they have looks solid.

On their first night, they drink a lot and then dance around the bare room without music. They are lighter than the others – when they walk the boards barely creak. They use more of the space, too, flinging themselves into every corner of the room. They sit first in one place and then another. They are moving all the time. They are touching all the time: if one leaves the room the other one follows soon after. They leave the bathroom door open and their dinner plates unwashed.

The windows are huge and black without curtains.

They have put up a shelf and they have done it badly. It is going to fall off. We know it is going to fall off. We can feel the screws loosening millimetre by millimetre. We can feel the shelf slipping. We knock off a book, then another book, to try to make them notice. They don't notice. The man picks up one of the books and reads out loud from it. 'Listen to this,' he says. We listen. The woman listens.

We don't like them very much. They look after each other more than they look after the house.

There is a night when, as if from nowhere, bright lights and flashes fill the house. We can smell smoke. Whenever this happens we think that perhaps it is the end of the house, but it is never the end of the house. They watch the flashes, their noses pressed up to the glass. They write their names in their own breath and their names stay embedded in it. We can see all the names that have been drawn on the windows, looped and layered over each other. We don't watch the flashes. We prefer to hide from them with our hands over our ears, waiting for them to stop.

They get a piano and put it in the empty room. He plays and she stands behind him with her eyes closed. The music spreads through the house like hot-water pipes. We have never heard noises like it.

They shower together before leaving in the mornings, slipping their bodies around each other in the water. It is like only one person lives here. Their dips in the sofa are just one big dip in the middle. They live with only one light on, in the one room they are both in. We straighten their shower curtain to stop it getting mouldy. We shouldn't have to do such things.

\*     \*     \*

The shelf falls. It makes us jump, even though we knew it would happen.

'How's the book?' he calls through from the kitchen where he is doing the washing-up.

She is reading, her feet curled up under her. 'Hmm? I already got milk,' she says, turning a page. 'I already got milk.'

He fumbles with a wet plate and water sloshes down his knees.

The shower switches on. It switches off. The man gets out, and after a pause, the woman gets in. The shower switches on and off again. This is much better. It allows the humid air to cool and disappear. This is much better. Maybe finally they are learning to look after the house.

They tread carefully and slowly – there is no jumping or dancing. They buy solid furniture. The lights are switched off earlier than usual and the television is on almost all of the time. They don't come back as early as they used to – they come home separately and later, sometimes covered in tinsel and glitter. They bring a tree into the house and we notice every needle that drops.

Other people come and they fold out a spare bed. They all sit together and look at the house. They have never paid this much attention. One of the new people is a curtain-straightener, a cushion-plumper. She insists on doing the dishes then purses her lips every time someone carries in another plate. When a bird crashes into the window she doesn't jump. She refolds the towels. 'The shelves you put up aren't straight,' she tells the man. She straightens out the shower curtain so it doesn't go mouldy. We like her very much and are sad when she leaves.

We have seen this before. All day, the woman has been pacing between the bathroom and the bedroom. Her steps are slow and heavy. She flushes the toilet and the pipes sing and hiss. Then she walks back into the bedroom, stands still in the doorway and then lowers herself on to the edge of the bed. Then she gets up again and paces. Then she lies down quietly on the bed. She is already carrying herself differently. We have seen this before.

The man starts coming downstairs in the night. He opens the fridge door and watches the light spill out on to his bare feet. Sometimes, he pulls open the front door and stands on the mat. The cold air rushes into the house. We shiver and get impatient. Why doesn't he close the door? He stands like that for a long time, until something makes him sigh and shut the door and go back upstairs.

The piano has disappeared. They have replaced it with a small bed and other noises and mess and lights clicking on and off, endlessly.

The boy is in the attic again. He is always in the attic now that he can walk up the stairs by himself. He is a small boy and he doesn't weigh very much. We know this because he fits easily through the hatch and he doesn't make the floor creak as if his legs will go through the ceiling. We don't have to worry about him going through the ceiling. He likes to be in empty rooms. He likes gaps and small spaces. Once, he hid (we knew where he was) and nobody could find him. A lot of people came to look. We knew where he was all along – inside the rolled-up carpet, for hours.

He has a tiny bird in a box. Three times a day he comes into the attic and leans over it. He puts little things in there. When he leaves, he pulls the suitcase in front of the box. 'Marty, Marty, Marty,' he sings to it. 'Marty, Marty, Marty.' This is what we have learnt from children bringing animals inside the house in boxes: never name them, never ever name them.

He stares at the box for a long time. Then he closes the lid and takes it away.

Conversations the boy has with himself, or with someone we can't see:
   Do birds sleep while they are flying?
   I am a ghost and no one can see me unless I want them to.
   If everybody else disappeared, would it be boring?
   He also sings, whistles, hisses, burps and clicks. He is like a miniature house.

Warm light comes through the windows and lies in slabs on the floor.

The buddleia is growing back. The woman comes up to the attic and tells the boy to go downstairs. She hasn't been in the attic for a long time. When the boy has gone, she does the strangest thing. She gets on to the rocking horse and she doesn't fall through the ceiling.

Brick by brick by brick, more houses are being built somewhere near by. When do we arrive in them? We don't know. Were we already there and the house was built around us? We don't know.

We don't exist without bricks and slate and glass, and bricks and slate and glass do not exist without us. There is no need to think about it any further, but sometimes we like to think about it a little bit.

The boy makes louder noises and puts more weight on the floorboards and stairs: bang bang bang. He doesn't go up to the attic now. He stays in his bedroom with the door and the curtains closed.

One day he disappears, but nobody seems worried this time. We can't find him anywhere in the house. No one else is looking. The house goes back to the way it was. There is only a toothbrush left behind in the pot, the banister he pulled off hanging askew. The house gets its quietness back; it gets its echoes and its quietness. Once or twice, the man goes into the boy's bedroom, talking, as if he has forgotten that the boy isn't there.

Things we miss about the boy who left:
The girl who came to visit him and wrote her name behind a corner of the wallpaper and then stuck it back down with spit.
The smell of the stuff he put on his hair – sometimes we would take off the lid and scoop out tiny little bits.

The house is bare. People come and go, mostly in pairs.

When they come in the front door, they bring with them one or two dry leaves, one or two variations of light, and then the door closes and the light is the same.

*   *   *

There are dark patches on the walls in the shape of furniture and pictures that aren't there any more. The rocking horse nods forwards. The carpet is thin and threadbare. Why doesn't anyone replace it? We would have replaced it by now. Light moves up the stairs and then down the stairs, and the house is dark again.

We miss lamps. We didn't think we would. We must have got used to them. At night, colours ebb away as if they were never there. The corners of the house darken and the hallway becomes narrower. A door bangs open and closed but we don't know which door it is. It isn't one of our doors. We would never bang our doors like that. It makes us nervous. We miss lamps. The windows are huge and dark. The curtains are still here, they usually take away the curtains. One night, we decide to close them. It is not our job to close them but we prefer it when they are closed.

At night, the house closes into itself and then it stills and quietens and sleeps, and we dream of it under water.

A strong breeze comes in under the door and chases us around the house. It slams a loose cupboard door. It furls and unfurls the corner of a loose piece of wallpaper in a bedroom. Underneath, someone had written something, which they shouldn't have done because that will be hard to get off and we can't remember who it was.

It's always the same – feet, feet, feet and dirt on the carpet and now everything is being moved, now everything is being changed. There is noise and there is more noise and then there is the worst thing: walls have been taken away and a door. Now there is a gap where the door was and there is a bigger room instead of two rooms and one less room where the wall was before. We have been rearranged. We hide behind the curtain poles and under the loose tiles in the kitchen. Things have been changed and things have been taken away. We are not sure. We are not sure at all. We have been rearranged. It is not what we expected to happen. How can you take away a wall or a door and not expect the whole house to fall down? How hasn't the whole house fallen down already? We cower, covering our heads, waiting for it to happen.

It hasn't happened yet.

The man who did all the moving and all the rearranging is staying here with a woman. They have put in a new carpet. We actually liked the old carpet. We actually miss the old carpet. They don't get up early and leave for most of the day like most of the others. Instead, they stay in bed for most of the morning and they eat breakfast in bed and get crumbs everywhere. We are not sure about them. But the woman sings in the shower and her voice is deep and beautiful, almost like the piano, and the man downstairs in the kitchen starts humming the same tune and it seems like he hasn't noticed he is doing it. They stand under the crack in the bathroom ceiling. They say it looks like an ear; they say it looks like a heart. Why are they so good at finding bits of themselves drawn on to the house?

We miss the piano.

They talk about things they are going to do to the house. They are going to get rid of the crack in the bathroom. They are going to pull out the buddleia. They are going to paint everything. They are going to rearrange more walls. We don't want to listen, but we have to listen. It seems like they have nothing to do except change the house. We push against the wall when they're drilling and break their drills. We cling to the wallpaper. It is our job to protect the house.

Now they have gone away and they have covered everything with sheets. We like everything covered with sheets. It keeps everything clean and less dusty. It is not our job to dust.

Sometimes we think of the butterballs. They are the only thing we have ever missed.

The new carpet is fraying. There is no stopping it. The buddleia is growing back. There is no stopping that, either.

Shadows that have passed across the keyhole: twelve.
    Number of silverfish in the attic: seven, but one is not moving.
    Dust that has floated past so far: four million, seven hundred and forty-eight pieces. There is a lot less dust than you'd think when a house is empty.
    Number of times we have banged into a wall, forgetting that things have been changed: too many to count.

We dream, and in our dreams, there are whole houses under water, and streets and trees. It is cold and quiet. Bubbles rise slowly out of chimneys.

They have come back. We think they are the same people but we are not sure. We are not good with faces. They seem much older.

They walk slowly up the stairs. They only take some of the sheets off the furniture. The woman stays in bed, not just late into the morning but for the whole day. The man lowers her gently into water. He sponges her back and washes her hair, keeping her propped upright. He is silent, he is concentrating hard. We, the house, hold our breath.

And we must have lost track of time because when we release it, the house is bare again. The rocking horse nods forwards. The air slows and stills in rooms. Nothing is ever exactly the same, but it goes back to how it was. We watch the door and wait for somebody to come through it.

# The Wishing Tree

THEY WERE LOST but it did look familiar. Maybe it was somewhere they had been lost before.

'I think we got lost here last time,' Tessa said. 'It looks familiar.'

Her mother, June, tapped the steering wheel with her nails and craned her neck forwards. She was almost sixty and had started wearing scarves all year round: she had summer scarves and winter scarves, all ironed into neat folds. She said to Tessa that it was because her age showed in her neck, but Tessa knew that she also wore them to cover up the small white scar on her throat. She had bought one for her mother herself – gold with red poppies on – and had sent it in the post, feeling complicit in something.

'So we're not lost. We know where we are,' June said. The roads were narrow with high hedges. She drove fast and every time they went round a corner Tessa braced herself against the seat, imagining another car coming straight at them. 'Stop doing that,' June said. 'You're making me nervous.' When another car did pass, they had to squeeze so far over that a kaleidoscope of nettles and bindweed pressed flat and star-like against Tessa's window.

'It looks familiar,' Tessa said again. They had come down here a couple of years ago so that her mother could visit an old friend and got lost trying to find the town. Tessa had been talked into going then and she had been talked into going again now. June didn't like driving long distances by herself and she needed an excuse not to stay at her friend's because she hated her dog, which clattered up and down the wooden stairs all night and left hair on the beds. 'We'll stay in a bed and breakfast and have a few days away. I'll pay,' she said. 'I've got vouchers.'

Now, Tessa definitely recognised that oak tree at the bend and the lay-by after it. 'Could you pull in here for a sec?'

June sighed impatiently, but she pulled in and stopped the engine. She didn't like stopping; she liked to be moving, on the move, even if she didn't know where she was going. 'I used to sit you on a newspaper to stop you getting car sick,' she said. 'I had to buy one especially.'

Tessa tried to open her door but the car was too close to the hedge. There was no way she could get through the gap; maybe a few years ago she could, but extra weight had started to creep up on her. Sean, her boyfriend of nine years, said he didn't notice any difference. 'You're just the same, aren't you?' he asked, gentle and puzzled as always. She put on his slippers and jumpers as soon as she got in from work and wore his baggy T-shirts to bed.

June got out of the car so that Tessa could climb over. On her way, Tessa knocked into the horn and it let out a short bellow. It was mid-August and heat funnelled into the lane. The mud was dry and packed down. There were bees everywhere. The hedges were full of honeysuckle and the hard green beginnings of blackberries.

There was a narrow path leading away from the road. 'I think we went up there,' Tessa said, although doubt niggled as always – she could walk back up a high street the way she'd come from and not know it, go back in the same shops.

June flicked a horsefly off the back of her hand. 'Where are you going?' she called.

Tessa's plastic flip-flops snapped against the ground. She remembered this. The path was overgrown and shady. There was a signpost with the top snapped off, thick ivy covering a gate; the ground was getting wetter and colder.

June caught up with her. 'If you see a horsefly on my back, kill it, will you? It's stalking me.'

The path ended suddenly and opened out on to a shallow pool of water with trees arching over. There, on the far side of the pool, was the tree they had found here last time. It hung low and wide over the water, its thin branches covered in hundreds of small yellow leaves and then, among the leaves, there were other things: a flash of red, something silver trailing almost into the water, a ribbon swaying from a branch. Up closer, the colours and shapes suddenly became hundreds of objects tied all over the tree: shoelaces, bracelets, plastic bags, plaited wool, gloves.

Everything seemed especially quiet and still. The water didn't move; not even one ripple.

'I'd forgotten about this,' June said.

Tessa nodded, although she hadn't forgotten. They had got lost here before and come across the tree, looking just as half-threatening, half-beautiful as it did now. It was like a strange bird crouched over. Tessa had heard something about wishing trees and knew it was one straight away, although somehow she had imagined it would have looked, or felt, different – more passive maybe, less like it was reaching outwards.

Last time, they had both made wishes. June had rolled her eyes when Tessa suggested it, but she looked at the tree for a while and took off the leather bracelet she wore around her wrist and hung it over a branch. Then she'd gone back to the car and sat in it with the engine idling, singing loudly and out of tune with the radio.

Tessa had taken the band out of her ponytail. She had looked back, heard the car's faint noise. She couldn't think of a wish. Her mind had emptied of everything; there was just her heart beating, just a vague tightness in her throat. She had thought it would be easy – why wasn't it easy? Nothing had come into her head, or rather, suddenly, this did: a memory of that morning when she had walked in on her mother after her shower. It was a mistake, an accident; it should have been something to laugh about. But June, who had wiped clear a gap in the fogged-up mirror and was looking at herself intently, sadly, whipped round like a startled deer, grabbed a towel, and wedged the door so it wouldn't open any further, peering round from behind it angrily. Afterwards, they had both pretended it hadn't happened.

That was it. Nothing else had come into Tessa's mind. It was ridiculous. She could never do anything properly. She knew that her mother was fidgeting around in the car, waiting to leave, so she had looped the hairband over a branch and stood back. What had she wished for, exactly? Nothing else had come into her mind. She had wished for nothing.

She'd tried to forget about it. Wishes she should have made flitted about like moths from time to time but she swatted them away. Maybe she would have forgotten about it completely, but now here they were back again.

'Where's the wish you made last time?' June asked. She had found her bracelet and apart from having faded slightly it looked exactly the same: it looked like a good wish, a solid wish. 'It's a shame it didn't work,' she said. 'They've stopped selling that design.' She had a magnetic bracelet on now which Tessa hadn't seen before.

Tessa looked for her wish but she couldn't find it. There was a Christmas tree reindeer dangling from one branch, a key ring tied over another. A lot of the thinner branches were bent under the weight of wishes. There was a ribbon that someone had written 'help' on and a daisy chain that had shrivelled and dried, each flower closed up tight.

June walked further round the tree. 'This glove's gone mouldy. There's mould all round the fingers.'

Tessa crouched low and looked up into the middle of the wishing tree. Then she saw her hairband. It looked like it had rotted. The elastic had erupted out of it and the whole thing was frayed, thin and crumbly. Her stupid non-wish had rotted. Her palms were hot and sweaty. All she wanted to do was take the band down off the tree and forget about it. She reached up and had barely touched it when it broke, one side falling away from the other. As it broke, she pulled her hand away because she felt something thick and invisible, as if she had moved her hand between two magnets. The band hung on the branch for a second and then fell into the water.

She stood up slowly, rubbing her knee, thinking 'that's that'. It was a comforting phrase and she used it a lot for cauterising loose ends. She turned back towards the car.

A breeze made everything on the wishing tree sway first one way and then the other.

'Got it,' June said, crushing the horsefly against her leg.

*   *   *

They stayed at the same bed and breakfast as last time. June said it would be easier, more convenient; besides, she hadn't had time to look up any others.

The reception was all dark blue and dark wood, with silvery paintings of snow and mountains on the walls. The carpet had big flowers on it, the kind that Tessa used to walk over by stepping on one flower at a time without touching the gaps. She did it now, stepping one flower at a time, although she didn't know she was doing it.

June took off her sunglasses and ran her hand across her eyes. She rubbed in circles over her eyes and her temples. Tessa watched her. She'd been rubbing over her eyes a lot during the drive. What were the next tests for again? Her mother had only mentioned it briefly, among talk of rain and what shoes she'd packed, and Tessa couldn't remember the right words. Still, it was nothing worth thinking about, she had definitely said that. It was only a precaution; they both knew it.

Magda, the owner, was on the phone. She looked over and gestured for them to sit down on the creaky wicker chairs. In the car, June had recounted all the things she and Magda had talked about last time – their allergy to bread; how Magda really wanted to work in sea rescue, winching people out of the water from a helicopter. 'Her ex-husband sounds like a maniac,' June said. 'He used to phone her up talking in an Australian accent.' She liked to hear about ex-husbands. Tessa's father had left a long time ago, but just before he did, he bought a chainsaw out of the blue and cut the bottom hedge into a bear that reared up on its hind legs, its paws flailing in the air. Her mother used to stand in front of it when she didn't know Tessa was around, watching it slowly grow over and disappear.

Magda put the phone down and June went up to the desk and smiled. 'Hi,' she said. She smiled a big smile, all teeth.

Magda said hello, smiled back politely and started the checking-in process.

'How's everything with you?' June asked, tapping the pen against the form she was filling in. There was a brass bowl filled with brass fruit on the counter.

'Fine, thank you,' Magda said. She took the form and checked it. 'And you?'

'Great,' June said. 'Great.' She twisted a short strand of her hair around. She dyed it mahogany, and her solid, cropped bob often looked like it was carved out of wood.

'Now, breakfast is between seven and nine. If you're allergic to anything you should let me know so I can try and find you something else.'

June stared at her.

'Do you? Have any allergies?' Magda asked again. 'It's just that I can't eat bread so I know what it's like.' She reached up for their key. 'I eat Ryvita now but it's not the same.'

Tessa saw her mother hunch her shoulders up slightly, making the thin shape of her spine visible for a second under her shirt.

'No,' June said finally. 'No allergies.'

Magda took them upstairs, walking slowly, once stopping to snatch at a cobweb, once to throw a feather out of a window. 'Here are your rooms,' she said. Her T-shirt had a thumbs-up printed on it.

'Rooms?' Tessa asked. They'd stayed in a twin last time.

'I booked us a single each. My treat,' June told her.

The rooms were small and each had a lacquered chest of drawers, a desk without a chair and a wardrobe carved with leaves. They both had a red plastic kettle and a mug with a photo of a Labrador on. Tessa's room smelled of bleach but there was a sea view – just – a tiny stamp of water between two other buildings. There was also a pencil drawing of the sun and the moon on the wall.

'We decided to keep that,' Magda said. 'It's vandalism, but what isn't?' She kicked at the carpet in the doorway to straighten it. She showed them their bathrooms, told them what time breakfast was again, and then left.

June bustled around Tessa's suitcase, taking out clothes, putting them on the bed and refolding them.

'This place must get busy,' Tessa told her. 'They must get hundreds of visitors.' She moved towards the window, which was dusty and the sun was hitting it, making it look like there was nothing outside except webbed light: no street, no other buildings, no window even.

'What kind of pyjamas are these?' June asked, holding them up.

'Oh,' Tessa said, turning round to look. 'They're Sean's.'

June pursed her lips a little, folded the pyjamas smaller and left them on the end of the bed. She opened the wardrobe to hang up Tessa's coat but the hangers were locked to the rail and she couldn't manoeuvre the coat on to one. 'Why would we steal hangers?' June asked. 'I find it offensive that they think we'd steal hangers.' She shook her head at them and then gave up, throwing the coat over the bed. 'Do you find that offensive?' she asked Tessa. Her scarf had come loose and she re-tied it, tucking one corner tightly into the other.

It was late afternoon and still warm. They followed the road into town. Most of the houses they passed were pebble-dashed bungalows, built for facing storms head-on.

Tessa wanted to find a café, maybe buy a newspaper. She liked to look at the photography – the country lit up at night, deserts, people – sometimes she didn't even read the articles, she just studied all the drawn, pensive faces. By now she would have had a mug of tea with three sugars after work; she had got used to tea at five and felt shaky without it. She worked at a garden centre, which was huge and sold everything from cactuses to chandeliers. She liked the sacks of dried beans and the rows of spades and vases. 'Where else can you get a cactus and a chandelier under the same roof?' she liked to ask people. She had worked there for years.

June wanted to go for a walk along the coast path.

'Are you sure you should?' Tessa said.

June stopped walking. 'Why not?'

Tessa took her purse out of her bag, looked at it and then put it back in again. 'It's just, is there enough time?' Her mother looked tired; she had that hard set to her mouth. A few years ago, they had gone on a day-long cookery course together and learnt how to spin sugar. They had to put their hands in ice before plunging them into boiling caramel. Tessa didn't trust that the ice would work, but June set her mouth into a hard line and did it quickly, coating her hand in boiling caramel and spinning it into a lumpy basket.

'We don't have any plans,' June said.

The road curved along the edge of the beach and started to rise up towards the cliffs. They went through a field with sheep grazing on the springy grass. The sheep looked up and watched them, scattering at the last minute. After the field there was another gate which opened on to the cliffs. The path ran close to the edge. There was gorse covered in tattered wool, thrift at the edges. Sand martins flew in and out of their nests, following the shape of the wind.

It was much windier up there than it had been in town. Tessa's loose trousers pulled back against her legs and then flapped out like a tent. There was a low fence where part of the cliff had eroded, but otherwise there was nothing between the path and the sea and she kept imagining the wind blowing her off – she didn't imagine falling, but rather being carried over the sea for ever without being put down.

June was walking ahead. She had always walked fast, pulling Tessa along behind her when Tessa was younger and they had held hands in busy streets. Suddenly, she stopped and leaned right over the edge of the cliff, so that it looked for a second like she was toppling forwards. Tessa's heart jumped into an uneven beat. She rushed over, her T-shirt sticking to her back.

'Look at that,' June said, straightening up. The waves were smashing and breaking on a line of rocks, throwing up huge plumes of spray. The rocks were a long way down. The sea glittered like fish.

'The cliff might break,' Tessa said. The drop was sheer, the rock smooth and striped burgundy.

'Cliffs don't just break,' June said. 'I'd know about it first.'

'You might not,' Tessa said. 'It might happen suddenly.'

'Look.' June jumped up and down twice. 'It's solid.'

'It could happen suddenly,' Tessa said again, wanting to grab her mother's arm and pull her away. She watched her jump again. A tissue flapped out of June's pocket and over the edge.

'Remember when you used to hide under the table whenever an aeroplane went low over the house?' June said. She looked down once more then rejoined the path. 'You thought it was going to crash through the walls.'

'That only happened once,' Tessa told her, although she still imagined it every time she heard an aeroplane. They came so close! She struggled to get her breath and talk at the same time. Her body felt heavy and difficult, unfamiliar. It felt as if someone had hold of her ankles. She could smell her deodorant wafting up, sweet and strong.

The headland leaned out like a boat. Up ahead, the path they were on forked and a smaller path sloped downwards towards the sea. June stopped and looked at it. 'We should go down there,' she said.

'It looks steep.'

'We should go down. There might be a beach.'

'There's a beach in town. Maybe we could go to that one?' Tessa said. The town beach was easy to get to from the road. There were other people. You couldn't get stranded on the beach in town.

June made an indecisive noise but veered on to the steeper path. She did that a lot: she would make an indecisive noise even though she had already decided.

It was hard to argue with her. When June had phoned that very first time, to say that she'd been into hospital and had to go back, Tessa had asked whether she should drive up and go with her. 'Don't drive all this way,' June had told her. 'It's absolutely nothing, it wouldn't be worth it.' Tessa couldn't remember the exact conversation; all she remembered was her pen pressing swirls on the notepad harder and harder and her mother's dry little breaths falling like snow into the receiver. She hadn't pushed it; she had taken her mother's word for it, had never just said: of course I will go.

Tessa put a foot out on to the path. It was steep and stony and difficult to get a grip on, especially with flip-flops. She took a step and a few stones clattered down and rolled past her mother, who was walking steadily with her body tilted backwards for balance. 'Wait up,' Tessa called. She tried to lean backwards too but every time she took a step her body would automatically lean forwards instead.

'Bend your knees,' June called.

How? Her legs refused to bend; they stayed straight and stiff and refused to bend. She skidded and more stones rolled down and her bag thumped into her shoulder. The whole cliff was swathed in pale heather which looked like a low-lying mist. It distracted Tessa, made her lose her focus. She tried to watch how her mother was walking, but when she looked up she skidded again. This time she couldn't find anything to grip on to with her feet and she fell down hard, pain jolting along the bottom of her back.

June looked back at the noise, hesitated for a second, then hiked back up. 'What are you doing?' she asked. There was a faint, shrill wheeze in her throat.

It felt like being a kid again, falling over. The ridiculous prickling of tears, the shock, stinging palms with stones stuck in them. 'It's steep,' Tessa said. Her ankle felt sore and she was hot and blotchy all over.

'Here.' June helped her up and dusted off the back of her T-shirt. She had strong, capable hands. Tessa had always assumed her own hands would change somehow when she reached thirty, becoming strong hands for brushing off backs and changing tyres, but they hadn't so far.

June picked Tessa's bag up and slung it over her shoulder. Tessa tried to put some weight on her twisted ankle, and found that she could walk if she swung her hip out with each step. It was slow going. The sea breathed in and out. The sand martins flew in curves. As they passed the town beach, the sun hit the wet sand at the tideline and lit it up like a copper pan.

Tessa lay in bed, drifting in and out of sleep. Her room was hot and she kept thinking she smelled smoke. She had opened the window and the curtains moved like someone dancing in and out of the room. Her ankle still ached; paracetamol hadn't touched it. In the corridor, there were footsteps and whispering – 'apples', it might have been, or 'unless'. A door opened and closed.

She bundled up the pillow and turned over. She had only ever spent a few nights away from Sean. He usually held her; he usually clicked his tongue as he was falling asleep, his mouth close to her ear. She put the extra pillow lengthways and lay with her arms and knees curled up to it but it didn't feel the same. She pummelled it and pushed it away and drifted into a light sleep, where images of bracelets and ribbons and leaves tangled into one another.

She was just about to fall into a deeper sleep when there was a noise from her mother's room next door. There was a crash, and then silence. Tessa sat up, listening. Nothing. Then, through the wall, she heard the creak of her mother leaving the bed. The fanlight clicked on in the bathroom. Tessa lay back down and waited, but the fan kept whirring and whirring and didn't click off.

Tessa got up and listened at the wall. She put her door on the latch and went out and stood in front of her mother's door. She heard a cough, and then a longer cough and then nothing. She knocked very quietly. There was no reply. There were two empty beer bottles in the corridor, quiet laughter a few doors away. She went back to her room and lay down. The fan clicked off. She heard her mother moving around the room. It sounded like she was picking things up and putting them down again, pacing. She paced around the room and went over to the window and slid it open. A few minutes later the TV came on softly.

After a while, Tessa drifted off. She woke up in the morning clammy and heavy-headed, the pillows rucked up and halfway down the bed and the duvet slumped on the floor.

*   *   *

At breakfast, June dug her spoon into half a grapefruit, skewering out each segment. Plates and knives clattered. Tessa dipped her toast in tea, leaving soggy crumbs in the cup. A couple at the next table were arguing quietly with their heads bowed together. 'You said you would turn it off,' the woman kept repeating, the conversation winding in tighter and tighter circles.

They didn't linger. They went out and wandered round bookshops and gift shops. It was hot and close and there had been rain. People brought the smell of the weather into the shops and bumped shoulders and shook out their wet hair.

Tessa held up a singing fish. 'Sean would love this,' she said.

'It looks tacky,' June told her.

'It sings shanties.' Tessa bought it and had it wrapped.

June wanted to try on jumpers ready for winter; she liked to be prepared. She used to buy Tessa's Easter egg half-price the year before.

She opened the changing-room curtain to show Tessa what she'd picked. The jumper was pale yellow and made her look completely washed out. The thin skin under her eyes looked bruised, her cheeks taut and shadowed. It looked as though she had lost at least two stone in weight. As Tessa shook her head at the jumper, she told herself that it was only the colour of it; no one suited yellow. And it was only the light in the changing rooms – everyone knew that the light in changing rooms made you look ill; it was a well-known fact.

June's friend Alice, whom she'd known since school, lived in a wide, leafy street on the edge of town. All the houses had huge bay windows, and it was easy to look in and see families having lunch, TVs flashing across walls.

Alice answered the door and kissed June on each cheek, then leaned back to study her face. She was tall and she wore heavy rings on every finger. The dog chased after June's feet as she went in and she grimaced and smiled weakly, didn't bend down to pat it.

There was a young girl in the kitchen. She had a streak of blue paint on her cheek.

'Amy's staying with us,' Alice said. 'Holly's away on business. I'll put the kettle on.'

Tessa sat down at the table, which was covered in newspaper and paintings of strange blue and yellow people, their long arms reaching off the page, their heads like pumpkins. The little girl came over, sat opposite Tessa and stared at her. June and Alice were already talking about old friends, people Tessa had never even met.

'You know what she's like,' Alice was saying. 'She shuts herself away. I hardly hear from her any more.' She went over to the fridge, looked in, then closed it again. She was easily distracted, constantly boiling and re-boiling kettles; Tessa remembered that from last time.

'I got a postcard so I thought she'd gone on holiday,' June said. 'But it was from her village, it had that church on it with all the gargoyles.'

Tessa had leaned her elbow in paint. She licked her finger and tried to get it off.

The little girl carried on staring. 'Come and see my castle,' she said.

Tessa smiled at her, not committing. She studied the paintings carefully.

'Amy loves showing off her things,' Alice said. 'I'll bring your tea up to you, Tessa.' She clicked the kettle on again.

Tessa had no choice but to follow the girl upstairs. They went into an attic room with a low, sloping ceiling. The bed was shaped like a butterfly. Tessa knocked into a plastic dragon on a shelf and caught it just before it fell. She sat cross-legged on the floor.

'Green tea, please,' she heard her mother say.

'Of course,' Alice said. 'Off coffee permanently?'

Their voices floated up the stairs, sometimes loudly, sometimes too quiet to hear.

'Do you like castles?' the girl asked. 'I thought you said you did.' She scowled at Tessa, flipping quickly into distrust.

'Sure,' Tessa said, trying to catch what they were saying downstairs. 'I like them.' She had never been good with children. Their sudden questions made her awkward, you couldn't just shrug them off; they looked at you without giving up. 'Why are you here?' a tiny boy in a duffel coat had asked her once at the garden centre. 'Why are you?'

'Mine is haunted,' Amy said. She moved a knight across the drawbridge.

Laughter from downstairs.

'We have to save Teddy the bear from the ghost,' Amy said. She shrieked and rattled the castle.

'Help,' Tessa said. She waved a horse around half-heartedly. 'Help me.' She tried to neigh but it didn't come out right.

'So sorry for you,' Alice was saying. 'Other things you can try . . .'

'. . . to find the cause,' June said. '. . . try anything. Doctors . . .'

Amy shrieked again.

'. . . I did read something the other week . . . a magazine . . .' Alice said. Her voice drifted halfway up the stairs.

Tessa put the horse down, unfolded her numb legs and got up. She wanted to hear properly. She made her way carefully past marbles and crochet hooks, an inflatable globe.

'What are you doing?' Amy asked. She looked Tessa up and down, cold and appraising.

'I thought the ghost might be out here, in the hall,' Tessa said. She stepped out of the door and stood at the top of the stairs.

'Don't be stupid,' Amy told her. 'I made that ghost up.'

'This woman,' Alice was saying. 'She swears by skinny-dipping in the sea . . . swimming . . . mixture of cold and salt, the shock of it, apparently. Transformative.'

June laughed loudly and then Alice laughed. The tap came on and crockery clattered in the sink.

'You should try it, though,' Alice said. 'Seriously.'

'I've got to show Grandma something.' Amy pushed past and ran downstairs and Tessa followed.

Just as they were at the door, June said, 'Well, why not? I said I'd try anything didn't I?' They both turned as Amy and Tessa came in.

'Tessa, your tea,' Alice said. She filled up the kettle. 'I thought of you the other day. I got a hyacinth, one of those ones where the bulbs are already planted in the pot.'

'We sell a lot of those,' Tessa said. Her thoughts raced.

'I can't stand the smell of hyacinths,' June said. 'They're like something rotting in a grave.' The kitchen smelled like paint, and rain began to hit the windows.

'I'll do it with you,' Tessa said suddenly. The words came out loudly and forcefully, as if she had just disagreed with someone.

'Do what?' June asked.

'The swim. The swimming.'

June looked at her. 'You heard that?'

'Oh, June, that would be perfect!' Alice said. 'Good on you, Tessa.'

June went over and examined some of the paintings on the table. 'I didn't think you would have heard that,' she said.

'I'll go with you,' Tessa said again. It occurred to her that this was something that would have to happen very soon, while they were still near the sea. She couldn't put it off. She imagined the waves and the cold water.

Her mother paused for a second. 'You should think about it,' she said finally.

Tessa thought about it over dinner. June picked at her lasagne but talked without stopping, ploughing through what she thought of the pub, what colour she wanted to paint her house, the flood she'd had a few years ago. She ordered pudding then took an hour to eat it.

It was late by the time they got back. Tessa sat on June's bed and thought some more. It was their last night. June had already said she wanted to leave as early as possible in the morning, beat the other traffic and the sun. Her right arm had burnt crimson on the way down.

Tessa kept her shoes on but June kicked hers off. She switched on the television. The sky turned dark blue and the street lamps came on.

'I'm going to do it,' Tessa said. She thought about lying in bed, listening through the wall as her mother paced restlessly. 'We have to do it,' she said.

June kept her eyes on the TV. 'You don't want to.'

'There's a smaller beach a few miles out,' Tessa said. 'I saw it on the map. We can drive out there.'

'You don't have to do it,' June told her. She laughed at the screen, at a comedian she usually hated.

Tessa got up and began to pack up a bag, towels and keys, sun cream. She took the sun cream out.

'You don't have to do this,' June said again. 'What if there are people around? Do you want to do it then?'

'I don't know,' Tessa said, wishing her mother would stop giving her ways to back out. 'We'll see.' She hadn't thought about other people. All she kept thinking was: this is my chance, while the rest of her bucked and thrashed, trying to make her drop the bag and turn away from the door.

June straightened out the bedclothes and put on her shoes and they left the bed and breakfast quietly.

The tide was right out and the sand curved towards it like a pale, grey wing. From the car park, the sea was a dark piece of cloth, fretting in the wind.

'We'll have to walk quite far,' Tessa said.

'If the tide was in we'd be doing it in the car park,' June told her.

Tessa had hoped that the car park would be empty. After all, it was one o'clock in the morning. It was one o'clock in the morning! She hadn't been out this late for years. There were two other cars parked there. It made her feel anxious knowing that somebody else was around somewhere. June said that it was probably just kids gone to get high in the dunes, but Tessa didn't find that reassuring; she kept glancing around, noticing every small movement.

It wasn't cold, or at least not as cold as Tessa had expected. In fact, it was strangely lovely. The rain had blown over. The air was full of late night smells: cooling tarmac, the sea, smoke, her own skin and clothes. And it was so quiet; there was just the sea in the distance and the marram grass rustling in the breeze, whispering and hushing itself. The moon dragged its bony body out from behind the clouds.

June shivered and pulled her coat tighter. 'I didn't think it would be cold,' she said. 'I thought it was meant to be summer.'

Tessa walked over the dunes and on to the beach. Her trainers flicked pale sand on to her jeans. She stepped on a sand sculpture of a turtle and quickly tried to remould it. She was breathing quickly and her heart was beating fast. Up ahead, she could see the tideline. It looked like a dark necklace. As she got closer, the necklace suddenly became hundreds of objects strewn over the sand: seaweed, plastic, twigs and feathers.

Further along, there was a dark line of rocks. She stopped behind it and put her bag down. A single cloud went across the moon.

Tessa undid her coat and put it in the bag. Her mother had a piece of hair pasted across her cheek. She was looking out at the water. The beach was empty, but Tessa wanted to check and then check again. She took off her jumper and her jeans.

'What are you doing?' June asked, finally looking away from the water.

Tessa skipped around in her shirt and knickers, trying to stay warm. 'What do you mean?' she asked. Her thighs were covered in goosebumps.

'Why are you taking everything off?'

She stopped skipping. 'I thought that's what we were going to do.'

'I didn't think you were actually going to do it.' June looked at Tessa's bare legs. 'Are you actually going to do it?'

'Of course I'm going to do it,' Tessa said, hurt. 'Of course I am.'

June couldn't get her watch off so Tessa unclasped it for her and put it in the bag. June unbuttoned her cardigan and unzipped her skirt. She took off her scarf, slowly, and Tessa glimpsed the scar on her neck, which was small and pale and curved like a mouth.

Tessa took off her underwear quickly and stuffed it in the bag. There. Her mother peeled hers off like it was an old, painful plaster. They didn't speak. Tessa walked forwards towards the sea.

Suddenly, there was a figure walking in their direction. Tessa clutched her mother's arm and they walked backwards fast until they got to the first low line of rocks and crouched there, naked and hiding. It was definitely a person, although it might have been a stone jutting out from the water.

June was kneeling, one arm flung across her chest. Her skin looked pale and fragile. Tessa could see the veins in her arms and the veins at the tops of her breasts like faded threads. Her stomach drooped a little and Tessa could see the shape of her ribs. The skin on her shoulders was puckered and sprinkled with freckles. She had lost weight; it seemed to have fallen away from her like a cliff eroding.

They were both crouching as low as they could behind the rock. 'This is terrible,' June whispered.

Tessa nodded. There was sand all over her – in the shells of her ears, in between each toe. In fact, it was wonderful. Most of the clouds had been blown away and there were the stars. 'I think we're OK now,' she said.

June waited a while, then slowly got up, rubbing at her knees and palms, which were stippled with sand indents. Tessa had thought that, at night, their bodies would become dark and secret and shadowy, that they would blend into the darkness, but here they both were, pale and glowing like beacons.

The sea was not a flat piece of cloth any more. It was a breathing thing: all legs and arms and lungs. It grabbed at pebbles and fumbled through them, dragging them back. The sand leading up to the sea was thick and wet, more like clay than sand. Each of their steps sank down an inch and then filled with water, as if they had never been there at all.

It was colder this close to the water. Every bit of Tessa's skin was crying out for her to turn back, to run away to the warmth of the car. She took a deep breath and walked into the sea. Freezing water sloshed round her ankles and up to her knees. She walked in deeper. She had heard it was best once you were in up to your belly, when you started to go numb. She could hear her mother walking in behind her – she heard her make a groaning noise as seaweed wrapped around her legs.

Tessa was getting used to the cold. Small waves slapped into her chest and arms. She waded forwards and soon she was up to her shoulders. She ducked under and swam. Her face was streaming and her hair had turned into a black, slippery rope. Her body sliced easily and lightly through the water.

She resurfaced after a wave and stared across the sea. For a few moments, she had completely forgotten about her mother. Tessa had drifted quite far out and June wasn't anywhere near by. The wind was picking up and lifting the sea into sharp peaks. She scanned the surface until she saw her mother struggling against the waves. She wasn't in deep water, but she was flailing around as if she couldn't keep her feet anchored down. She fell and her bottom rose up like a jellyfish. Tessa swam back until she could wade. She caught June and lifted her so that she was standing.

'It turns out I can't swim very well,' June said, not really looking at her. Her voice was thin and husky. Water bubbled out of her nose and mouth. They were both goosebumped all over. Tessa held her mother's trembling body upright. Wave after wave swept in, still small, but the force of them kept knocking June backwards. 'I don't think it will work, will it?' she said. The sea had washed off her make-up and it looked like the bones in her face were fighting their way to the surface. 'I haven't done it properly, have I?'

Tessa looked down at her mother's wet face. 'I don't know,' she said. She supported her mother's body and started half walking, half floating her forwards. The water took most of her weight. June shut her eyes and gripped Tessa's arm as each wave buffeted in. They got into deeper water and then stopped. She clung tighter, but tried to lean forwards. A wave hit her and she spluttered and coughed and hacked up salt. Her arms chopped weakly at the surface. Tessa helped her mother move through the water. Her small body felt weightless, untethered, and Tessa clung to it and held her up and didn't let go.

# Blue Moon

I GOT DOWN on my hands and knees and snatched at Mrs Tivoli, but she darted under the bookcase and cowered there, pressing her quivering haunches against the wall. Her eyes rolled and she let out a yelping scream that cut into the room and sent tight, cold waves running up and down my skin. 'Come on, Mrs Tivoli. It's all right. Just relax.' She pressed in harder and her fur rasped against the plaster. I looked around and saw that the bedroom door was slightly ajar. You could still hear the faint, slow footsteps of her visitor going down the three flights of stairs towards reception. 'It's OK,' I said, trying to be soothing. 'You just stay right under there, Mrs Tivoli. Right under there. I'm just going to sit here and wait.' Then I launched myself towards the door and clicked it shut. Just in time, too, because she was already mid-run at it – her long, muscular legs pushing hard against the floor. She stopped, looked wildly around the room then rubbed over her ear with a shuddering hind leg. I leaned back, trying to think about my next move.

There's a detailed procedure for handling events of this kind but I have to admit that, at the time, it flew right out of my head. The only step I remembered was to seal off all doors and windows. It's policy for staff to log all transformations, noting events leading up to the change, possible causes, length of time in metamorphosis – the extra admin is a drag but what job isn't swamped in bureaucracy these days? This was the first time I'd seen Mrs Tivoli change into a hare, though, and the logbook doesn't have any entries for her. Some of the other residents do it if the kitchen runs out of ketchup or they miss their favourite programme on the telly, but Mrs Tivoli wasn't like that. She was usually so composed, so self-contained, as if nothing could faze her at all.

Blue Moon Nursing Home opened just over four years ago. It was the first of its kind, set up to cater for the demographic banned from regular establishments. When news of it went round there was a flurry of applications from all over the world. We got enquiries from Fiji, Cuba, and the Ural Mountains. Locals got priority, though; it paid to be in the right catchment area. We were full from the first day, with a waiting list that could have filled it again three times over. It's a brand-new place with all the mod cons. Research showed that buildings with a history could have a detrimental effect: residents can be sensitive to lingering voices, emotions and events that embed themselves in walls. The fresh paint, MDF and the rubbery smell of new carpets seem to have a calming effect. It's one of the reasons they want to come here.

As with any new establishment, it took a while for everyone to get settled. At first, the place was chaos – you couldn't serve tea without someone turning it into blood or oil, and they were always in and out of each other's rooms stealing wax and recipes. We kept finding them down at the harbour trying to sell the wind to fishermen in lengths of knotted rope. Our vacuum bags filled up with soil, twigs and fingernails. It was a nightmare cleaning out whatever they'd been mixing in their baths; bleach wouldn't touch it. We'd scrub for hours, the stuff corroding away six pairs of rubber gloves, hearing faint shrieks coming from the smears.

Although most residents came here planning to retire, they didn't seem to know how. In the first few months the home was full of anxious or bereaved locals wandering around looking for help and burying scraps of old beef in the garden. We had to curb practising hours to Thursday afternoons and patrol the kitchen to stop anyone filching potatoes and salt. There weren't clear enough regulations about familiars either and none of us knew what to do with them, so they tore around the corridors and fought each other for territory. After that it was keep it in your room or lose it and mostly they stick to the rules.

I'm on reception but I do a bit of everything: cleaning, food prep, general care. Residents hardly ever get ill, which is one of the perks. I lock up after my evening shifts and make sure everything's secure. It's a comforting final task, going round re-enabling the smoke alarms and checking the fire escapes. Most of the time the work here is easy – everyone gets into a routine. The salary makes up for the difficult bits: finding dead men's hands festering at the backs of cupboards; the smell of fox and badger shit lingering in your throat. People at my old place thought I was mad when I applied here but now most of them are kicking themselves that they didn't do it when they had the chance.

Reception's usually quiet except for Thursdays, when I book in their appointments, but even that's slowing down now. Some have their regulars but people tend to forget about them once they've been in here a while. Personal visits are rare. I'd say on average most of them are visited about twice a year, usually by a grateful local, an old neighbour or a nervous relative. When somebody gets a visit pencil-led into the book you can feel the jealousy oozing under the doors and soaking into the carpets.

Mrs Tivoli moved into 3B just over a year ago with her catfish, Maria. She insists on being called 'Mrs' even though there's no evidence of a husband and she never talks about one. Still, all the residents have their quirks. I'm inclined to believe it's because it made her feel less lonely; we've all got to deal with it one way or another, but who knows? It's not our job to go asking questions. Her eyes skip between dark brown, green and grey. She's short, shorter than me even and I'm no willow. Her silver earrings are longer than her hair, which is thick and bobbed and a deep chestnut colour. She looks about thirty-eight but I'd swear to all sorts of gods that she was at least seventy. Applicants have to state their age before they come to Blue Moon but I've always said it's a waste of time – they don't have a clue so they just guess. None of them have any official documents. They just keep themselves in as good shape as their powers allow. The girls in the kitchen joke that it's all right for the residents, they can fix themselves up without touching dye or surgery. Yet, despite what they look like, their bodies and minds are giving in to most of the usual symptoms of old age. At first it's unnerving, seeing healthy-looking people lowering themselves gingerly into chairs, clutching at banisters and forgetting words and faces, but you get used to it. Mrs Tivoli had a nasty fall which broke her hip just before she moved in and now her legs are trembly and uncertain; she walks with a stick and drops off in her chair after lunch with her head nodding into her cleavage.

She seemed to take some sort of a shine to me right from the start. We do the crossword together during my tea breaks and sometimes she lets me scatter Maria's colourful food pellets into the water. If I get a bout of thrush she clears it up for me no problem. The staff handbook advises not to get close to residents. It says that they can easily use you, manipulate you, but most of us think that's a load of rubbish – half of them don't even know where they are. Mrs Tivoli barely leaves her room. She still has her old things scattered round – a hand mirror made of thick, black glass, a string of wrinkled conkers, lumps of clay going dry at the edges – but they're slowly getting covered over with other things: marzipan wrappers, glossy magazines, TV remotes and biscuit tins.

A couple of months back, I was tidying her bedroom while she was down at breakfast when I noticed one of the drawers under her wardrobe was open. We don't go in residents' cupboards, we only tidy what's out, but I thought that I might as well straighten up inside just this once. I suppose I didn't want to go back down to the desk and the silent telephone, my pad of acrostics. I looked around. Maria was staring right at me from her tank. She's an odd-looking thing: she doesn't have scales, just this thick skin covered in mucus. I didn't even know there were fish without scales. Now that she's getting older, her whiskers droop against the pebbles and her skin is flaking off in soft scabs that rise to the surface of the tank. Mrs Tivoli scoops them out with a tea strainer and keeps them in a jam jar.

'I'm just dusting,' I said to her. 'Nothing to fret about.' I opened the drawer out a bit further and Maria thrashed her tail like a mop. Inside, there were rows of bottles bedded down in newspaper: cleaned-out milk bottles, those HP sauce bottles with the slim necks, and small gold-capped ones from baking ingredients like vanilla essence and food colouring. They had white labels stuck to them. I flicked the duster around even though there didn't seem to be a speck of anything in there. Lots of the labels had dates on them; others said things like 'St Michael's graveyard', 'R. Tavey', 'Withheld information', 'Mother'. I've picked up plenty of bits and bobs since working here; I could name most of the things that Mrs Tivoli keeps in jars on her shelves – arrowroot, yarrow, mandrake, curled mint – but I didn't have a clue what was in these. The stuff inside looked grey and feathery, like ash from a bonfire but heavier somehow and more liquid. I glanced back at Maria. She was watching me very carefully. I shut the drawer.

I went back to 3B during my afternoon break. Mrs Tivoli was watching the home-shopping channel. 'Fifty pounds for that piece of junk?' she said. 'That's robbery, daylight robbery.' I remember thinking that she'd been looking tired for the past few days; she wasn't eating very much and I'd caught sight of one or two crinkled grey hairs along her centre parting. 'Look at this.' She gestured at the screen. A bronzed man was holding up a plastic mixer. 'Do you know how much he's selling that for?'

I shook my head.

'Twice as much as it's worth! And some chump will phone in for it, mark my words.'

I settled down in my usual chair and unfolded the paper. 'One across,' I read out. 'Eight letters. Extremely hungry.'

Mrs Tivoli glanced at me. 'Maria says that you cleaned one of my drawers this morning.' Maria pressed her suckered mouth up to the tank in a fat, brown kiss.

Snitch, I thought. Out loud I said 'starving' and wrote it in, although later it turned out to be 'ravenous'. 'It was open. I gave it a quick dust.'

She nodded, still watching the screen. 'How's your finger?' she asked.

I'd got a nasty burn off the toaster that morning before work. 'It's nothing,' I told her.

She pointed to a vase of swan's feathers on the windowsill and I picked one out and brushed it three times against the burn.

'I was going to show them to you anyway,' she said, carrying on from before. There was loud clapping from the television and the name of the caller who had bought the mixer flashed up. Mrs Tivoli pursed her mouth and switched it off with the remote, then put her hands flat on the chair and lifted herself up slowly. I knew by now not to ask if she wanted any help. She went over to the drawer and rummaged around carefully. The bottles clacked together like tongues tutting. She mumbled to herself as she did it: 'not that one, not that one, too much, too strong, not enough time.' She picked one out, came back over with it and handed it to me. It was a medium-sized vinegar bottle and it was strangely warm. It might even have been pulsing but it was probably just my own hands because I was suddenly nervous. The label said 'Rita Adams'. 'Open it,' she said to me. My hands lingered on the cap. 'You know that it's against the rules for me to take part in your work, Mrs Tivoli.'

She sighed and rubbed a hand over her painful hip. 'You're not taking part in anything,' she said. 'You just have to watch.' Her bracelets rattled. 'But if you're uncomfortable maybe you should go back downstairs.'

I unscrewed the lid. The air in the bedroom seemed to contract and move, as if a huge line of washing had billowed out and then been snapped backwards by the wind. Mrs Tivoli muttered something and the bottle got warmer. I waited. Nothing else happened except I noticed a strange smell that I could have sworn wasn't there before. It was a damp, earthy smell, like a pile of wet leaves or a very old jumper. It could have been overripe fruit but there was a bitterness to it that I couldn't place at all. The bottle cooled down in my hands and another woman appeared in the room. She was hazy. Her body looked watery and brown, as if she had been cut out of a sepia photograph. She was tracing the bobbles and dents in the wall with her index finger and had a vacant smile on her face. The woman, Rita I supposed, looked like she had been beautiful once, but now she was lopsided and awry. She wandered round the room with unfocused eyes and her head tipped to one side. She tripped over my chair and laughed soundlessly as she clawed the hair out of her eyes.

After a few minutes Mrs Tivoli muttered something else and the woman vanished. I closed the lid and took a deep breath. If Mrs Tivoli was summoning ghosts into the establishment I'd have to take it further.

'Rita's not dead yet,' she said, leaning her head back on the chair.

The staff handbook advises us to close any conversations that could lead into uncertain territory. 'What was that then?' I asked.

'I used to know her,' Mrs Tivoli said. 'She lived near me. Everyone who saw her fell in love with her. One of my customers suspected her husband was having an affair with Rita and she asked for my help. I was in a rush. I had hundreds of things to do and I didn't do the work properly. It got messed up. She wasn't meant to turn out how she did.' She shrugged. 'Still, c'est la vie. We didn't like each other anyway.' She was breathing a little more heavily than usual and she kept smoothing her dark eyebrows over and over. I had no idea what she was talking about but I smiled and nodded at her reassuringly. I didn't want her getting upset. She frowned. 'Everyone has things that follow them around,' she said sharply. 'Mistakes, regrets, things they wish they'd done or hadn't done. It's far easier to put them some-where you can keep track of them, stop them sneaking up on you. Don't you think?'

'I suppose so,' I said, thinking suddenly that mine didn't so much sneak up on me as linger around chest level.

Mrs Tivoli reached over to her wheel-in table and picked up a box of marzipan fruits. Her fingers hovered over it like a pair of moths while she chose which one she wanted. She's addicted to sugar but her teeth are perfect. She offered the box to me but I shook my head. It was past my break by then anyway and I didn't want to get into trouble with the duty manager.

That afternoon seemed to start something. Over the next few weeks, whenever I paid Mrs Tivoli a call, she would have picked out one of the bottles to show me. It would be there on the table, waiting. If she expected me at any point and I'd had to work over my shift because of some crisis or other, she would call reception on the internal line. 'I was just wondering whether it was time for your break?' she'd ask casually.

'Gloria has gone AWOL again,' I'd tell her. 'It's all hands on deck.'

'She's locked in the supply cupboard in the basement,' she would say. 'She was looking for arsenic.' So then I'd be free to go up and see her.

I saw planes without Mrs Tivoli on board take off through the bedroom ceiling. I saw her give away one of her most treasured possessions (an extremely rare strain of seaweed from the Dead Sea) to someone who didn't appreciate it. I watched her dig up a shallow grave at a set of crossroads to steal a silver bracelet, the reek of the grave slamming right into the room. 'Never rob the dead,' she said to me, shaking her head at the image of her younger self wielding a huge spade. 'It's a tricky business and never as useful as you'd think.' I saw short, awkward meetings with her distant mother. I saw her pour away a bowl of gold liquid straight into her garden, turning the grass and the trees black and steaming. At one point she opened an old milk bottle and a black and white film flickered across the wall. Apparently she'd only ever watched the first half of *Citizen Kane* even though everyone said it was the best film ever made. 'Maria hated it,' she told me. 'She said that it was just a bunch of men slapping each other on the back.'

I gradually realised that the smaller the bottle was, the stronger, more potent the feeling trapped inside. Mrs Tivoli was keeping mainly to the bigger ones, though, and leaving out all those small bottles I'd seen in the drawer. I was glad about it, relieved even. The smallest one she had ventured to show me so far wore us both out in a second. We watched as she placed her hands over a young girl's stomach, while the girl squeezed her eyes tight shut. I shuddered into my armchair and Mrs Tivoli looked so exhausted I was tempted to call in the nurse.

After that one it was back to medium bottles but I knew from the glimpse of them I'd had that they must be running out. I couldn't get that young girl's face out of my mind and had almost decided to ask Mrs Tivoli to stop when I walked in a few days later and saw a tiny nail-varnish bottle on the table. The lid was scarlet and the label was blank. Mrs Tivoli and Maria had their eyes fixed on it. Neither of them looked up at me. I didn't sit down. 'I can't stay,' I said, stopping in the doorway. 'There's a thing I have to do downstairs.'

Mrs Tivoli kept her eyes on the bottle. 'Please,' she said. When she unscrewed the cap the smell was instant and overwhelming. It was so strong that you could almost see it draping itself over the room like a dust sheet. I've gone over and over it since and the only way I can describe it is this: if homesickness had a smell then it would be that one. My eyes burned with it.

A man appeared in the room. This time, the image was so defined that I could see colours and contours. There was nothing flat or hazy about him. I could see every stitch on his green jumper. He looked like he was in his late thirties and he had dark brown hair that was sticking out in messy peaks at the back. There was something on his cheek that I couldn't quite make out at first; it could have been a cut or a shadow. The man stared at Mrs Tivoli for a few moments then smiled sadly and went towards the door. He looked back once, fumbled with the handle and then walked through it. The whole thing played out so quickly that I nearly missed it. After he had gone, Mrs Tivoli didn't move an inch. I leaned forwards to close the bottle for her but I couldn't bring myself to touch it. The image appeared again. We watched him walk out of the door three times before Mrs Tivoli dragged her hand up and closed the lid.

Over the next few weeks we went back to our normal routine of crosswords and cookery shows during my breaks. Mrs Tivoli's eyes kept straying away from the TV and falling on certain points in the room: the door, my chair, somewhere near the window. I was always ready for her to start talking about what she'd shown me, but she never did. 'It's cold in here. Don't you think it's cold?' she would say instead, tucking a blanket around her legs. It wasn't cold at all. The heating would be on and clunking away through the radiators. Most of the other residents had turned theirs down.

'It is a bit nippy,' I'd tell her, and she would nod and ask me to make hot chocolate, so strong and sweet it would make your teeth ache.

I was spending more time away from reception. Most days the phone wouldn't ring at all so I was roped into doing extra cleaning. There had been a spate of pentagrams appearing on the common room carpet, marked out in salt, and I had to hoover them up. It's a real pain because the grains bind themselves to the carpet fibres and won't shift unless you keep a pinch of salt on your tongue. By the end of it you're parched.

Normally I wouldn't miss anything when I was away from the desk but yesterday was different. When I got back, the appointment book was out. One of the porters or the nurses must have taken a call for me. I flicked through to see who had a visit scheduled. It was Mrs Tivoli and she had a Mr Webb booked in for the next day.

I didn't sleep well last night – I kept seeing planes wrapped in green wool, a swan's feather caught in a spider's web. When I got into work this morning I stayed on reception without budging. Mrs Tivoli had never had a visitor before and there was no way I was going to miss seeing who he was. Mr Webb wasn't booked in for a specific time, though. That's the problem when someone else does your job for you – they don't ever do it properly. You're meant to specify an exact time for the visit so that everyone can be prepared. I ate my sandwich at the desk and didn't even leave to go for a wee. I just clenched and tried to forget about it. By mid-afternoon I thought he wasn't coming and my shift was about to finish. When he finally walked into the lobby my bladder almost gave out. He had the same face, the same hair as that man I'd watched leaving Mrs Tivoli's room just a few weeks ago. He came up to the desk and I signed him in, trying all the time to maintain my professional veneer, trying not to stare at his green jumper or the small shaving cut on his cheek.

I took him up to Mrs Tivoli's room myself and knocked on the door. While we waited, I smiled at him and found myself bobbing at the knees. I'm better over the phone than face to face, I'll be honest, but I think I just wanted to calm him down, he looked so apprehensive. He was tall and skinny, and when I say skinny, I mean skinny so that his face looked gaunt and shadowy. He had dark, heavy eyebrows that frayed out at each end. They made him look as if he was constantly frowning, but there were laughter lines radiating out from the corners of his eyes. I kept having to wipe my sweaty palms on my blouse and it seemed like hours before Mrs Tivoli called him in.

She'd tidied and changed the room around – her slippers and blankets had gone and there was a throw covering the television. She'd brought her telescope out and set it up by the window and her almanacs were stacked up in place of the magazines. There were also three chairs in the room. I didn't know where she'd got the other one from. She gestured for both of us to sit down. I stared at that third chair and then up at Mrs Tivoli. 'I'd better get back,' I told her.

'You've finished your shift,' she said.

I sat down. My heavy bunch of keys clanked at the belt of my skirt. Mr Webb glanced over but didn't say anything. I backed my chair quietly into the corner and huddled down in it.

Mr Webb went up to Mrs Tivoli and bent over her head. As his lips lingered against her hair she closed her eyes, just for a moment. He pulled back slowly and then wandered around the room, picking things up and putting them back down again. He went over to the shelf where she keeps her wrinkled potatoes stuck full of pins.

'What are these for?' he asked.

'You know what they're for,' she told him.

Mr Webb picked one up and turned it over. 'I thought you weren't going to do that any more,' he said.

She shrugged. 'Now and again.'

He put it back down quickly. 'This is a nice place,' he said to her. Next door's toilet flushed and we heard muffled footsteps and the creak of someone sitting down on a bed.

'Maria thinks my room has damp,' she replied.

'Everywhere's damp to Maria; she lives in a bloody fish tank!' he said and laughed like he was gasping. He cleared his throat. 'How is she, anyway?'

'You never liked Maria,' Mrs Tivoli said to him.

'We had our differences,' he said, gesturing at the tank. Maria picked up a stone and spat it out. 'I told you I would have got used to her.' His jumper sleeve was fraying and he kept pulling on the loose threads so that it unravelled more. 'She's not looking quite as sprightly these days.'

'Time marches on,' she said.

'Not for you, though,' he said. He looked at Mrs Tivoli intently. His profile was so angular, so hollowed out, that there was something almost beautiful about it. 'Soon I'll overtake you.'

Mrs Tivoli sat stiff and regal in her armchair. She'd hidden her walking stick and her pain-relief medication. There was a single rune on the table.

Mr Webb started to pace around again and neither of them said anything for a few minutes. 'I've been transferred,' he said finally.

Mrs Tivoli turned her neck slowly and looked out of the window. There were goosebumps on her bare arms. 'Yes,' she said.

'They're opening a new research centre. They want me to run it.' He sat down in his chair and leaned forwards.

'What will you research?' she asked.

'Weather systems,' he said. They looked at each other.

Mrs Tivoli tilted her head to one side and frowned slightly. 'Don't you already know everything about those?' she asked.

'They're always changing,' he said. 'You know that. And they vary. We've done all the work here so now we need to look further afield.' He looked like he was going to carry on but he stopped himself. 'Anyway, I've got a few more days to decide about it.'

'Does this have to be in Scotland?' Mrs Tivoli asked.

'We need somewhere that gets a lot of rain,' Mr Webb said. He didn't seem surprised that Mrs Tivoli knew where the job was.

'It rains a lot here, this close to the moor,' she said.

Mr Webb sighed. 'It's to do with the mountains. We need to chart the specific volume and the density and . . .' He trailed off, rubbed across his eyes.

'The rain in Scotland is full of despair,' she told him.

He unfolded himself out of the chair and stood up again. 'That's what I . . . That's the reason I came you see. If I didn't go . . . I came because . . .'

She shook her head quickly and interrupted him. 'You have a small wart coming on your left hand. You wanted me to remove it.'

He looked down at his hand and rubbed over the palm. He looked up and back down again until Mrs Tivoli beckoned him over. He knelt down in front of her. He breathed out slowly. She took a pin out from behind her ear and asked Mr Webb to reach over for a jar. She blew on the pin for a moment then took his hand and eased the pin into it. He winced. She looked steadily at him as she moved it in a circle. Maria had turned her tail on the room and was facing the wall. The bubbles in her tank streamed out and broke on the surface.

'That window looks a little draughty,' he said. He rested his cheek against Mrs Tivoli's thigh. 'Do you get cold?'

'Not often,' she said, circling the pin.

'I could look at it for you. I could come over in the next few days and look at it for you,' he said.

She sighed. 'There are porters.' The pin circled like a clock's hand. Mrs Tivoli held Mr Webb's hand in hers, which was plump and smooth but riddled with invisible arthritis. Nothing moved for a long time except the pin. Then Mrs Tivoli blinked and seemed to come to. She slipped the pin out, breathed into the jar and dropped it inside. You could see her breath winding around in there like a trapped storm. Mr Webb raised his head reluctantly and Mrs Tivoli shifted. The weight must have been hurting her bad leg.

'You remember what to do with it?' she asked. He said that he did. 'It'll be gone in a few days. You'll never know you had it.'

Mr Webb backed into his chair. Mrs Tivoli glanced at him, then closed her eyes and tipped her head back.

They were silent for a while and I wondered whether it would be possible to sneak out. I felt as if I could barely breathe. I had imagined myself creeping out so many times that, as time passed and nobody spoke, it was almost a surprise to find that I was still there in the room.

'I need to ask you something,' Mr Webb said after a while. 'It's important. I think it's important.'

'I don't think it's as important as you think,' she said.

'But it is.'

'When you go to Scotland,' she said, 'something will happen to you, something good.'

He shook his head.

'I've seen it,' she told him.

He glanced over at her black glass mirror. 'I told you not to,' he said. 'It doesn't mean anything.'

'It does mean something.'

'Well it doesn't matter,' he said. 'Look at you. Nothing's changed.'

This time, Mrs Tivoli shook her head.

Mr Webb put his elbow on his knee and cupped his face in his palm. 'It doesn't mean anything,' he said again, but more quietly this time. A wind chime caught the trace of a draught from under the door and clacked its hollow wooden legs together. Nothing else in the room moved for a long time. When Mr Webb got up to leave he kissed Mrs Tivoli on her pale forehead. She kept her eyes open and her neck very still.

'It's for the best,' she said. It wasn't clear exactly who she was addressing.

Mr Webb tucked his hands deep into his pockets. He smiled at Mrs Tivoli, then walked towards the door, looked back once, fumbled with the handle, opened it and walked through into the corridor. He'd left his fogged-up jar on the floor.

I wondered if Mrs Tivoli had forgotten I was there and I thought I'd better get up and leave her alone. We listened to Mr Webb's slow footsteps as they crossed the corridor. Mrs Tivoli was sitting very still. She looked tired and older than I had ever seen her before, as if another body had risen up underneath her skin. She stood up after me and brushed down her skirt and I noticed how much her hands were trembling. Her eyes were going wide and she was breathing heavily, heaving her chest and shoulders up in big movements. Her feet tapped quickly on the carpet and then it happened before I had a chance to do anything. Her shoulders dropped right down so that her arms were dangling towards the floor. She slumped on all fours; her chest stiffened and seemed to cave in and then extend again into a tight, rounded drum. A sudden coating of brown fur moulded itself over her clothes and skin, as if a bristling layer of iron filings had been magnetised on to her. Her hair scattered silver clips and split into thick halves that sprang up on top of her head in two black-tipped ears. She shrank in seconds and crouched motionless against the floor. Then she snapped into frantic, hysterical movement. She scrabbled over the bookcase and the bed frame, upsetting books and digging pale marks into the wood with her claws. Her first scream was like nothing I've ever heard. I didn't think anything was capable of making a noise like that – it sounded like it should have cut her stomach and throat to pieces on the way out. It made my spine clench and the backs of my eyes sting. That's when she got under the bookcase and I noticed the door was open.

After I'd slammed it shut, Mrs Tivoli quietened down a little. She stopped in the middle of the carpet and nibbled it, still shuddering, still breathing in deep, heaving groans. I was expecting the closed door to have an adverse effect. I was expecting it, but I didn't know what to do if it happened. I was meant to have pushed the assistance button by now but it was on the other side of the room and I should have placed a substantial object between us. I didn't care about that, though. I had a terrible fear that she would try to break out through the double glazing, bruising and battering her frail body. But she didn't. She bowed her head down and seemed to gather back into herself. We looked at each other and as her eyes shifted from brown to green I realised why she had needed me here. She knew that Mr Webb would leave the door open. She must have watched him do it a thousand times before she showed me. She knew that she wouldn't have any control over herself, so she needed me to be the one that closed the door and sealed her inside. I felt heavy and sick. I stayed leaning against the door and watched as she lifted her nose and sniffed the air, mapping out her room, her world, in ways I couldn't even guess.

# Wisht

*(adj.) melancholy, pale, lonely.*
*The wisht hounds run across the moors*
*hunting the lost and the dying.*

THERE WAS NO torch blinking its way back towards the house. No arm and then body followed behind. No click of the gate and footsteps along gravel. It was the same every night that he went out, which was often. She would lean on the windowsill and stare outside, waiting. If she left the light on, a pale version of her room hung behind the glass – her walls, her clock, her desk – see-through and only half familiar. And inside that other room, her own small face leaning forwards to look back in. When she turned the light off, she couldn't make out anything beyond an inch of the window, then, after a while, shapes would emerge: a fence, a hedge, trees. There were fields and then there was the moor, stretching away like a strange blanket. That's where his torch would come from, when it finally appeared. But for now it was just shapes behind darker shapes.

She always pretended to be asleep when her father came in to check on her. The important thing was not to stay too still; she made sure she rolled over, or kicked out a leg or mumbled into the pillow. But he still talked to her as if she was awake. 'I'm going out,' he would say, standing in the doorway. 'I'm locking up.' Then after a while: 'I won't be long.' Once he had gone, she would get up and go downstairs. His glass would be on the draining board, empty except for two lumps of ice. The fridge light would glow green in the dark kitchen. He might have left the TV on mute and she would sit in the narrow dent he had left behind and watch whatever came on.

After a while, she would go back upstairs and start waiting at the window. Her stick insects would be asleep inside the tank. If she tapped the side, their legs and antennae would open out like leaves searching for light. She had three. Her favourite was Cat Stevens, who always escaped. Often, he would end up on the back of one of the chairs in the kitchen and her father would almost squash him when he leaned back. 'Wait!' she would shout. 'There's Cat Stevens.' And he would jerk forwards as far away as possible and wait for her to pick him up. 'He's OK,' she would tell her father. 'Look. He's OK.'

'Cat Stevens was a fucking genius,' her father would say, bending his head down towards a newspaper, towards coffee.

'Look, he's all right.'

'A genius,' he would say again, and he would shake his head slowly and lean back in the chair.

Sometimes she would fall asleep with her cheek on the shiny paint, sometimes with her forehead pressed against the glass. Sometimes she counted the gaps where she had lost teeth with her tongue: one, two, three; another wobbly and tough as a carousel horse.

Most nights she heard the wisht hounds howling across the moor, maybe following her father, maybe further away than she thought.

189

What did their howling sound like most? Like the wail a cloth made when you wiped wet windows. He had told her a story about them once, about how they stalked across the moor, and now she heard them almost every night and she was sure that they were following him and that soon they would catch up. 'It must be the wind,' her father said when she told him that she had started hearing them. 'Moors are windy. It was only a story.' But he couldn't back out of it now – the wisht hounds were one of those things she had always known existed, she just hadn't known the name or the shape of them. It wasn't as if she believed any story he happened to tell, but the thing was, whenever she was lying in bed and the night seemed to stretch on for ever into the distance without ending, or when, on the edge of the moor, there were hare's bones or narrow, arcing tracks through the long grass, then it seemed quite obvious that this story was true.

'I know it was only a story,' she told him. 'I know.'

'Jesus. It's only a story.'

She glared at him, narrowed her eyes and didn't tell him when she heard them again, or about the deep scratch that had appeared at the bottom of the gate.

When her head fell forwards against the window, her short hair brushed the corners of her mouth. It never stayed behind her ears even though she kept tucking it there. She tucked and tucked her hair. The clock ticked in odd rhythms. A few times, when her father came back, he had come upstairs and hung wet clothes over the bath: trousers soaked to the thighs, shoes dripping river water. The clock sounded like his clothes dripping dry over the bath.

Tucking her hair, the clock ticking, sometimes she got so tired that all she could do was crawl into bed and sleep before he got back. But most nights she waited and the whole night would be black in front of her until his torch appeared in the distance, a fleeting flash like a cat's eye or a kingfisher, so that she wasn't sure at first whether it was there or not. Then, it would move closer and the light would bob around and get bigger until finally she could see her father behind it, walking through the field. Then she was in bed and practically asleep already by the time he came in the door and stumbled around, banging cupboards and glasses and cursing quietly and tiredly under his breath.

This night was different, though. He came in the front door and went straight up the stairs and knocked softly on her bedroom door. She was almost asleep and the knocking got into her dreams and she thought it was somebody hammering a nail into a wall. 'What picture?' she asked.

'Are you awake?' her father said. He came into the room and sat on the side of her bed. 'Are you awake?' She opened her eyes and looked at him. He was wearing his jacket and his shoes. 'Come outside. I want to show you something.' He rubbed at his cheek and when he spoke there was the grey tooth among the white ones. It was grey and maybe getting darker. A dying tooth.

'What?' she asked. He smelled sour and smoky and of sweat. 'What?' she asked again. He got up off the bed and wandered around her room, picking things up and studying them: her harmonica, her cactus. He touched a leaf on her mimosa and it bowed downwards. She had gone on a school trip a week ago and asked him to water it but he must have forgotten because this was a new one. She could tell because there was no yellow leaf at the bottom and there was a pink flower out when there hadn't even been a bud before.

'Your plant,' he said. 'A flower.'

She nodded and swung her legs out. It was cold out of bed. Her pyjamas were too short and stopped before her ankles and they were starting to stretch across the chest so that her belly showed. Her duvet fell off and her father put it back on the bed. She swayed, almost asleep standing up, so he picked her up and carried her. She hadn't been carried in a long time. They went down the stairs slowly; sometimes her head grazed the wall, sometimes her back. Her face was pressed up against his neck. His skin smelled of the hair products he used at the barber's. His hair was combed back; if you touched it, it was hard like plasticine. There weren't any bits that stuck out or felt soft. It was light brown hair, fading to nearly colourless, and it smelled like candles. As she was being carried, she ran a finger across the straight, neat line at the back of his hair, lightly so that he wouldn't notice. He had some deep lines in his cheeks and a pale row of chickenpox scars on his forehead. He was thin and wiry and not very tall. He had a split down his thumbnail that had never healed and his hands felt dry because they were always in water or on wet hair or had wax on them.

Her father cut her hair. He wrote her name in the appointment book just like anyone else's, first name and surname. The appointments were usually straight after school or on a Saturday morning. The barber's shop was a small room with one chair in front of a mirror and a sink. The lights were bright and one always buzzed but never got fixed. The floor was chequered in black and white tiles. In one corner there were two white tiles next to one another because there had been a mistake. Only men went in there to get their hair cut. There were two more chairs next to a low table full of newspapers and magazines and a tray with a kettle and a jar of coffee and three mugs. Whenever she went in there, the men would lower the magazines they were looking at and put them face down to try and hide the topless women on the cover. Then they would shuffle around and grin and touch the backs of their necks and ask her questions like what did she want to be when she grew up, or what was her favourite food, big questions that you should only ask someone once you knew them very well. 'A chef,' she would say quietly. 'Toasted cheese sandwiches.' She hung her bag and her coat carefully on the stand.

He put her down at the bottom of the stairs, among the shoes and umbrellas. There was a wooden triptych hanging on the wall, three birds engraved in three trees. It came with the house. Her father had moved it to cover a shallow hole in the wall that hadn't come with the house. He looked at it while she put on trainers. He checked his watch and then told her she would need a coat. She looked at the coats lined up on their hooks and then she looked up at her father. She took one of his coats, a grey woollen one, and put it on. It reached past her knees and her arms were lost inside the sleeves. He opened the front door and they went outside. While he locked it, she rolled up the sleeves of the coat. They walked through the gate and then across the road and into the field. Her father walked quickly and she had to run a few steps to catch up. He put his hands in his pockets. She put her hands in his pockets. Inside, there were two coins. She asked him how come they were outside; did he remember it was school tomorrow? She had a project. 'There's something,' he said. 'Rich told me about it at the pub. I'd forgotten it was tonight.'

It was cold and damp and windless. Everywhere there was the memory of wind in the fraying edges of things and the stooped-over branches. The field was full of holes so she had to slow down, walk looking at the ground. Up ahead, her father stopped suddenly and swore and shook his foot around. 'Watch out for cow shit.' She caught up and followed behind him, putting her feet where he had put his feet. The field was wet and sometimes his feet left a shallow, watery print. The prints were narrow: he had thin, narrow feet.

'You're thin,' she said. His thinness had been on her mind for a long time. He hardly ever seemed to eat. One of his shoulders lifted up but he didn't say anything.

Now that her eyes were used to the dark, it was much easier to see – it hardly seemed dark at all. It was strange. She thought it would be darker outside at night, but the night actually looked darker from inside the house. What the night was was this: shapes that were pale and shapes that were dark. The track was paler than the rest of the field; there were pale stones in the grass; the hedge they were walking towards was darker. There were shallow trails of water through the grass and they were pale and gleaming, and then one bigger spill of water and, inside that, two or three stars. She looked up and saw that there were more than two or three stars, many more, thousands of them, hanging above their heads in patterns. She stood still, staring.

'Come on,' her father said.

'I didn't see them before,' she said.

'They've been there the whole time.'

She carried on looking up. The stars spread over the whole sky, over the whole moor.

'Come on,' her father said again.

He walked on, towards the end of the field, and she followed.

'How many stars are there?' she asked.

'I don't know.'

'Millions?'

He side-stepped something and then checked his watch.

'Millions probably,' she said.

'Probably,' he said.

She caught up and walked next to him and their legs walked in a pattern, left, right, left, right. Then there was the open gate at the bottom of the field.

There were stories about people disappearing. Last year there was that woman, and before that, a man. No one could remember their names or what they looked like but everyone knew someone who knew someone who had known them. 'They don't even leave the skeleton,' kids said at school. 'That's because they don't eat them, dumbass.' 'What do they do, then?' 'I dunno. They don't eat them, though. It's something else.'

What her father said was that people leave places for more reasons than she could understand. She had been going on about it for days and he hadn't said a word. Then he just came out with it: people sometimes leave quickly, you wouldn't understand. It didn't sound right – why would they? It was evening, lights on and curtains open, and she suddenly pictured their house from the outside – small and fragile, the lights barely reaching into the dark, like a tiny boat in miles and miles of water.

She liked it best in the barber's when there was no one else there, when there was just the radio playing too quietly to actually listen to, so that, once in a while, a stream of music would reach unexpectedly into your ear. When it was her turn, her father would nod to her and take down one of the black capes and wrap it twice around. Inside it, she felt crackly and static. He would raise the chair while she was sitting in it and she would watch in the mirror their faces getting closer together. She wondered if they looked similar. He would spray her hair with the plastic bottle of water until it was wet enough to cut. The water was not too warm, not too cold. Above her head, on the ceiling, the bobbly paint looked like a woman's face, just one side of it, her hair in a low bun, her eye heavy-lidded and sleepy, her mouth in an almost smile.

The gate was as far as she had been for years. She was all right if she went the other way – there was the town and the river. She didn't mind going that way. But she hadn't been past this gate for years. There was a deep patch of wet, churned-up mud separating the field from where it turned into the outer border of the moor. Her father started to walk around it, keeping to the dry edge. She heard howling – a sudden thin noise that bowled across the grass.

'There,' she said.

Her father kept to the dry edge. There was another howl and he paused, ever so slightly, as he took a step. Then he carried on and was over the mud.

'There,' she said again. 'You heard it.' She waited on the other side, the howl still in her skin.

'What?' he asked. 'What?'

She pulled the coat tighter. The sleeves had unrolled but she kept them that way, her hands lost somewhere inside. Maybe they would go back now. She waited for him to turn around but he carried on walking. The night shifted itself to cover over his thin body so that in a matter of moments she couldn't see him. She waited. She imagined the wisht hounds galloping along like the shadows of clouds.

'They're not even real,' she said. It came out as a whisper. But what if they were out there? He shouldn't walk around by himself like he did, and he didn't eat enough either – there were dark spaces under his cheekbones. She had heard of people losing their energy and not being able to walk any further. She tried to make him eat more sometimes, but he just shook his head and looked past her at the TV, picking at his food, one foot jiggling restlessly.

She stood waiting for him to turn around and come back for her. Once, he had told her to phone up her gran for a chat, tell her how school was and about her plants. She had never liked using the phone and she dialled too quickly and when someone answered she said, 'Hello, is that Gran?' and the woman on the other end said yes it was, and it was a minute before she realised it wasn't her gran she was speaking to, it was someone else's. Her father was watching her speaking and she spoke about school, about her plants, about her stick insects, and waiting on the phone for the woman to say goodbye was how she felt now, standing by the gate, although she didn't know why.

She looked back towards the house. All the lights were off, except for the bathroom light which shone out of the tiny window. Now and again, headlights passed on the road. She could turn round and go back, wait on the doorstep. She looked ahead. It wasn't as dark as she had thought it would be. And their feet had walked in patterns. She didn't want him to be alone with the wisht hounds. She went through the gate, keeping to where her father had walked. On the other side, she picked up a stone as big as her hand.

She walked in a straight line from the gate and hadn't gone far when she heard a noise. It was someone laughing. There were two voices. One voice was her father's. She gripped the stone. It had a rough edge like a tooth. She stood a little way away from the voices and after a while the other man saw her, and he stared and he carried on talking. They talked in low voices to each other and they laughed a lot, but not the kind of laughing where you knew they were talking about something funny. She had seen the other man before, in the barber's, reading the paper, swirling strands of hair around on the floor with his foot. Straight after a haircut, his ears stuck out more and there was a pale band of skin along the back and around his ears. His wife had fooled around. That's what she heard in the barber's, that his wife had fooled around, but it didn't seem like anything to mention.

'Where were you?' her father asked, but he didn't seem to expect an answer.

'Maybe she had to take a leak?' the man said. He was drinking something from a bottle and he offered it to her father, who reached out and took it. She didn't go any closer.

'I didn't have to,' she said.

'So I told him that if he thinks that pile of rust is worth that much, he's got another think coming.'

'He should scrap it. He should just scrap it.'

'That's what I told him. But he won't hear it. He's sentimental is what he is.'

'I didn't have to,' she told them again.

They passed the bottle between them. 'He should scrap it. It's a pile of rust.'

'That's what I told him.'

The man kicked at the ground to dislodge a stone. It came out muddy and there was a streak of mud on his pale shoe.

'He hit that horse with it, didn't he? I thought he would have got rid of it when he hit that horse but he didn't.'

'I forgot about the horse.'

'Yeah, the horse. Said its knees buckled like an airer. He said sometimes he can't stop thinking about it.'

She stared at her father. 'We had to hurry before,' she said. It was cold and damp and windless. He gave her a look. He gave the bottle back to the man.

'I don't know how it didn't get written off.'

She went up and stood close to his sleeve, which she knew annoyed him but she did it anyway.

'I wanted to get up to the point,' her father said.

'Maybe I'll join you,' the other man said.

She pulled at her father's sleeve. He reached his arm up, away, to touch his hair.

'Yeah,' he said.

'Nice one.'

She felt a flash of hatred for him, for both of them. They started walking but she wanted to turn back. She trailed behind. It was too late to go back now. Everything looked the same to her; the ground looked the same everywhere but her father seemed to know exactly where he was going. They didn't notice her trailing behind so she caught them up because she didn't want to walk by herself. She walked out of sync with her father but wasn't sure if he noticed or not. The other man whistled badly.

The moor was dotted with granite boulders and clumps of longer grass. It smelled damp. It smelled big and cold and lonely, like the moon might smell. The slopes were getting steeper. Her father told the other man he wanted to stay away from the mires further down.

'Jesus Christ!' the man said suddenly. He swatted at his face. 'A fucking bat was this close, this close.' He showed how close with his hands.

'Bats don't hurt you,' she said.

'That was too close for my liking,' he said. He took another drink. 'You know something I heard about bats? I think this is right anyway.

They know the smell of the house or the barn they got born in, and they go back there and if they can't get in because the chimney or the windows are boarded up, they bang against them and fly against them because they have to get back in.'

'Why?' her father asked.

'I don't know. That's all I heard about it.'

'Like moths looking for light,' she said. She pictured those bats flinging themselves against a barn, trying to get back in.

'Yeah, I guess like moths,' the man said. Her father was quiet.

The ground was rockier. There were humped shapes all around. Her father tripped and fell on to his hands but he didn't swear. He told her to be careful even though it was him who had fallen.

When he started cutting her hair, thin slivers would fall on to the floor around her feet, dark at first and then drying lighter and splitting into hundreds of scattered pieces, like salt or stars. He tried to be careful around her ears, because once she told him it hurt when he combed over them. He put an inch width of hair between two fingers and straightened it out to get the right length. She could only feel that he was touching her hair because she could feel the pull on her scalp. She wished that hair had feeling. Why didn't hair have feeling? It would hurt too much when it got cut, she supposed. That was why. He always cut too short, so that her hair wouldn't stay behind her ears and so that some of the girls at school said she looked like a boy. She had started smuggling a silver clip in her school bag. She had found it under a loose corner of carpet in the bathroom. She kept it with a cake tin she'd found at the back of a cupboard and an old tin of mandarins, which she knew her father would never have bought, and a packet of sweet-pea seeds, years past the use-by date.

She put the silver clip in her hair just after she left the house in the morning and took it out before she got back.

Sometimes he hummed songs she didn't recognise; mostly he was quiet.

She watched her hair falling. The scissors made a noise like crickets. 'All right?' he would ask from time to time.

'All right,' she would reply, listening to the noise like crickets.

She wished the other man would fall over and roll away into the dark. He was breathing loudly and couldn't walk that fast so he was slowing them down. She had no idea where they were going. She was walking in front now, keeping her head down and listening to where her father was walking to make sure she was going the right way. She listened and heard him stop, so she stopped and waited. 'Just checking this is right,' he said to the other man. He looked around and then nodded. It all looked the same to her. What if they were lost and he was just pretending that he knew where he was? She was sure that no one could tell. There were slopes and rocks, and sometimes big rounded rocks like people hunched over. 'We haven't got long till it starts.'

There was another low howl from the distance. She saw her father and the other man exchange a look then the man shoved his hands in his pockets and started whistling again. She hated it – they were keeping it, that, whatever it was, everything, from her. They shouldn't even be out here. 'We could stay here,' the man said. 'It won't make any difference.'

'I wanted to get up to the point,' her father said.

They walked uphill some more.

'I would have had it off him if it had been cheaper,' the man said.

'You wouldn't want it with a dent like that in it.'

'He should pay someone to take it off his hands.'

'What happened to the horse?' she asked.

'I thought he got the dent sorted, actually,' the man said.

'He did a bit. But you can see it in the paint. It's right there in the paint.'

'Was the horse OK?' she asked.

After a while her father said, 'I don't know.' He checked his watch. 'Shit, we've only got a few minutes.' He looked up at the sky. 'Maybe we should just stop here.'

'For what?' she asked.

'I don't know if we'll have time to get up there.'

'It'll be just the same from here,' the man said. He had already sat down, and then after a moment he lay back with his hands behind his head.

'I wanted to get right up this bit,' her father said. 'To the top.' They looked around for a patch without too many rocks. Her father kept looking up and he didn't sit down. The man closed his eyes and started to snore, quietly and with a faint whistle. There was only that noise now in the whole night. She didn't want to be here next to it; it seemed a shame to be next to the only thing making a noise in the whole night.

Her father looked down at him and then he looked up the slope. He gestured for her to follow and he turned quickly and scrambled to the top. At the top, there was a pointed finger of granite and then a flatter piece. They lay side by side on that and stared at the stars which had been there the whole time. They were like faraway torches. 'Any minute now,' her father said. 'This is good, eh?'

She nodded. She hoped her father wouldn't go to sleep. He closed his eyes for a moment and she felt as if she had been left alone and the house and her bedroom and her father were all somewhere very far away. Then he opened his eyes again. It was funny how he had managed to find his way here when sometimes he banged around the house because he couldn't find the scissors or the bin bags.

She was cold. She moved a bit closer to her father. His elbows stuck out behind his head.

'At school,' she said, 'we did a project.' After a moment she said, 'The stars aren't really there, are they?'

'How do you mean?'

'Because they're not really there. Because they're in the past.'

'Yeah. Light takes so long to get to us. So those stars we're seeing are the stars from years ago.'

She nodded. 'What are they like now?'

'I don't know. Maybe the same.'

He was thin. And his hair and his shoulders. They were silent for a while. 'Orion,' he said. 'The dipper. Cassiopeia.'

She looked at him.

'Constellations,' he said. 'The patterns. Leo. Canis Major. Draco.'

'Leo, Canis Major, Draco,' she said.

He pointed them out to her. The names of the stars seemed to come out of him like some old, half-forgotten language. She looked at him, and had the feeling that something was continuing on without her. They traced the shapes in the air. The stars and the shapes were scattered across the sky and she echoed the names as he said them.

'There was one,' he said. 'I think I just saw one.'

She looked and then saw two stars fall out of the sky, trailing a brief silver thread behind them. Then there were more stars moving, dropping like spiders. They faded slowly into the black sky like ink being absorbed into paper. It was as if the whole sky was dropping stitches, unravelling itself ready to fall and drape over them like a blanket. And she lay there, looking up, and as each star fell closer towards them she thought: that was the best one so far, no, maybe that one,

   no, that one
      that one
         that one.

# Some Drolls Are Like That
# and Some Are Like This

*The wandering minstrel, story-teller and newsmonger . . .*
– The Drolls, Traditions, and Superstitions of Old Cornwall

MID-SEPTEMBER AND THE GEESE were back. The droll teller saw them as he wandered slowly down the street, following the same small route he took every morning. They flew in over the cliffs, calling to each other, their voices like harmonicas. The droll teller was hundreds of years old and he had seen the geese fly back hundreds of times, but every year he stopped and watched them, thinking about the distance they had travelled to get back to this same place, thinking about the Arctic tundra nestled in their feathers, the strange map they carried with them in their bones and feathers. Except this year he couldn't remember the word for tundra, and he couldn't connect the geese to the Arctic – he had no idea why, when he thought of one, he thought of the other. He also had the vague, unsettled feeling that they were arriving early, although he couldn't remember when they usually arrived, and so after a while he just watched them and didn't think much at all.

He saw Harry coming along the street towards him. Harry was up and around early, which meant he'd probably locked himself out and spent another night at the harbour looking at boats. If he was lucky someone would have given him a sandwich, thrown him a blanket.

'Locked out again?' the droll teller asked. He had never owned any keys. He'd found a buckled tent a few years ago and slept in that, which was better than sheds and benches, no one to rage at you as soon as you'd got settled.

'The key's gone,' Harry said. He always stood too close, so that you could smell his sour clothes. The services had finally given him a flat to live in. It had a TV and a hotplate. He wasn't allowed guests.

'You'll have to get Jack to pop the window. If you can find him.'

Harry glanced back down the way he'd come, then leaned right in. 'Those people there,' he said, pointing.

The droll teller looked. There was a man and a woman standing at the end of the street. They were in their fifties and he thought they were probably tourists. They were looking around as if they were waiting for someone. The droll teller always used to be able to recognise tourists, because he'd known everyone that lived in the area. Hundreds of years of people and they'd all greeted him by name. He had been the centre, although he wasn't sure of what, exactly. His name, his name – no one had said it in a long time and he grasped at it, came up with nothing.

'So what?' he asked. Harry was getting more and more suspicious and probably thought those people had stolen his keys. He said there were hidden cameras spying on him in the flat. The droll teller had known Harry for years, could recall him as a boy, in fact, all bones, always hungry. They used to borrow Jack's boat and go out night fishing. There were a few images that sometimes flashed up: a body tangled in a net; closing a man's eyes softly; drying their clothes around a fire; a torch cutting through trees; rain on an old car roof; rifling through straw; doors closing hard; bolts drawn.

But, come to think of it, he wasn't sure that he'd done all of that with Harry. He'd known a lot more people than just Harry – people came and went; it was hard to tell one from the other. Faces became other faces. And they had all gone the same way: forgetting, becoming ill, weak, boring, giving up the struggle, while the droll teller had stayed more or less the same, watching it all, getting left behind. Except maybe now it was different, maybe now it was his turn to go through all that.

'I heard Meg's got hold of some good stuff,' Harry said. 'Crates. She needs to shift it quickly.'

'Well?' the droll teller asked. 'What are you telling me about it for?' He felt his temper flare up, but not much; it was mostly embers now. He wanted to go and see where there might be food. Hoban had said he could go round to his workshop and watch TV later, his favourite programme was on and Hoban often had slices of pizza, the kind with meat and pineapple. He was good for waiting around with, passing time.

'Those people there,' Harry said. 'They're waiting for that story tour.'

'They'll be waiting a long time.'

Harry nodded. 'They'll be waiting a long time, I should think.'

'A long time.' And then after Hoban's, the droll teller thought, what would he do after that?

'Season's over. The tosspot that runs it has gone on holiday.' Harry looked at the droll teller, his eyes almost closed with old sun-glare.

'It's crap,' the droll teller said. He'd watched that man a few times, smiling with his sharp mouth, wearing a green top hat, checking his watch as he talked.

'It's a tenner each person,' Harry told him. 'Cash in hand.'

The droll teller looked up.

'It's all the old stories,' Harry said. He started taking his shirt off. 'Wear my shirt, it's cleaner.'

The droll teller looked down at his top. Someone had given it to him. It smelled like last night's chips and the sleeves were unravelling. Underneath, his skin had dried out and hardened so that it was almost like wood. There were grainy cracks and furrows etched all over it. The tendons in his arms and hands had tensed and thickened like branches; they had been like that for as long as he could remember. A tattoo on his forearm had worn down to pale smudges – it could have been a mermaid, or someone's name. There were only a few faint marks left.

'All the old stories?' he said.

'It'll be piss easy,' Harry told him. 'We'll go to Meg's after.' He held out his shirt and shivered, even though it wasn't cold. He'd already forgotten how to be surrounded by weather. His skin was getting thin and pale – no more brambles and barbed wire.

Down the street, the man started to pace and check his watch.

It had been a long time since the droll teller had thought about any of the old stories, even longer since he'd told them. 'Give it here then,' he said, putting on the shirt. Meg got hold of good quality. He could already taste it; a few bottles would pass the time.

'An hour,' Harry called after him.

What was the point in an hour? The droll teller used to tell stories that lasted weeks, spinning them out night after night, weaving everything together. They used to beg him to keep going; the pub would stay open till morning. They would give him a warm bed and more food than he could eat.

The couple watched as he got closer. He caught a glimpse of himself in a shop window, knew there was something of the scarecrow about him. It had been a long time since he'd been to that woman's, the one who let him use the bath. She had kind hands and soap that smelled like summer. He'd let himself slip more and more, feeling like something was coming to end, that finally, somehow, things were ending. He tried to smooth his matted hair and beard as he walked over the cobbles.

Tourists usually looked bored, as if they felt they had to do things and see things but were just waiting for them to be over. The two people at the bottom of the road looked desperate for the tour to start. He was almost half an hour late – anyone else would have left by now, secretly glad they could browse round gift shops instead. The woman got up from the wall as he approached.

'You here for the tour?' the droll teller asked them.

The woman nodded. She looked relieved. 'We didn't know if it was still going ahead,' she said. 'With us the only ones.'

Her hair was dyed red-brown like conkers. She smiled at the droll teller and a web of lines appeared around her eyes. The man's hair was solid and black and his shirt was tight across his belly. They looked as if they had just had a good, big breakfast, lots of butter and coffee. The woman reached into her bag and the man reached into his pocket. They both brought out wallets at the same time.

'It's still on,' the droll teller said.

'Do you want this now?' the man asked, holding out money. 'Or at the end?'

'I'll take it now.' The droll teller folded it carefully into his pocket then pushed it in deep. He'd had a note whipped out by the wind once.

'Can we get a receipt for that?' the man asked.

'I don't think we need a receipt,' the woman said.

'Is it possible?' he asked.

'I don't do receipts,' the droll teller told them. He was sick of this already.

'Forget it,' the woman said. 'We don't need one.' She shook her head slightly at her husband, then brushed something off the sleeve of her coat. They were both dressed up smartly, strong perfume mixing with harbour smells. The man's shoes were long and shiny as cars. They didn't look comfortable, unlike the droll teller's boots, which were worn in just right from the miles and miles of walking he used to do. He'd found them on a beach one winter.

He turned right down an alley and the couple followed him. Rows of whitewashed cottages backed on to each other; there was only a narrow gap. A few bins were out. Most of the cottages were empty year round, except for a few weeks in summer. He'd squatted in a couple of them, found them cold and stale. He could see the blue flames of a gas heater in one window. He'd always been drawn to hearths and fires. They used to keep the fire going all night at the pubs and houses he visited, if the story he told was good enough. They could get through a whole tree. He'd had his own camping stove once but someone had stolen it. There was no point looking for another one now. His boots creaked like gates. He walked slowly and now and again he would let out a long breath through his nose which whistled quietly, like a breeze through a gate.

'We're going to end up at the mines, aren't we?' the woman asked. 'For the last story?'

'The last story,' the droll teller said. A black cat jumped up on a wall, its body fluid, like water gathering back into water. Black cats. He automatically looked at his palms, at the lines printed there, but there seemed to be too many. There were thousands of lines, crossed and re-crossed over each other.

'The tin mines. I think it said on the poster.'

There was a story up there somewhere. 'Beware you who go to the mines at night . . .' the droll teller said slowly. 'Who said that?'

The couple glanced at each other.

'I don't know,' the man said.

'More words come after,' the droll teller said. He could see the words but he couldn't put them in any order. He stopped trying. The music from his favourite TV programme started playing in his head. *When life is hard, I know that you'll be near me.* He led them through the network of alleys.

After a while the woman said, 'This is a lovely area.'

'We had to come down anyway,' the man told him. 'We thought we'd stay on a few extra days.'

'No point hurrying back to an empty house,' the woman said. She laughed and it echoed off brick.

Why were they telling him all this? He hated it when people talked about this place when they knew nothing about it. Did they sit hour after hour watching drenched palm trees in the churchyard? Did they know how to avoid the kicks and the sticks if they strayed into the wrong area? Did they know the difference between how the streets sounded now, with all the traffic and the building work, and how they had sounded before? Did they have to force themselves to get up, day after day after day here?

'Day after day,' he muttered to himself. 'Day after day after day.'

September always had clear light and big, mackerel skies. The droll teller could smell cold, wet clothes from a washing line, and inside a house, someone was calling, plates were clattering, cupboards slamming. He had no idea where they were, needed to get his bearings. It was happening more and more. He wondered how far they were from the main square. He saw a set of steps leading down to a basement. They reminded him of something – what was it? He stopped. They all stopped and looked at the steps. There was a story associated with those steps, he was sure of it, some kind of ghost in this alley.

'See those steps?' he asked. 'A hundred years ago, on a dark and stormy night, there was a murder there.' He thought about the details. They would want it short and easy, they would want a storm. 'A woman, Jane Lyons, had been cheating on her husband. Whenever she could, she would sneak through the streets to that house there and meet with her lover.' It was coming back to him now. 'Her husband became suspicious. He was a violent man, a drunk, and one night after she left the house, he hid and followed her. He confronted her. There was an argument and he threw her down the steps and she died there, at the bottom.' The couple looked down at the spot, half expecting blood. 'And to this day, people swear they still see Jane Lyons hobbling around, her back broken, searching for her lost lover.'

Even as he was finishing, the droll teller realised that he'd used a plot from a soap he'd watched at Hoban's a few weeks ago. A husband had discovered his wife's affair and killed her by pushing her down some stairs. It had been a good episode. Hoban's chair had cracked when he'd leaned back on it. He'd fallen asleep and when he'd woken up there was a coat over him.

He looked down at the steps, shook his head, muttered something about roofs, or shoes. The shoes were important: he could see a shoe snagged on a hawthorn bush somewhere; he could see a tree with ribbons tied on it, small yellow leaves, but the right story wouldn't come, the parts wouldn't join up. So, he had let the stories slip away. They weren't buried anywhere. He thought they might have been buried somewhere. He realised now why the world had become flat and empty. Things were ending. He felt, what did he feel? Scattered perhaps, stretched thinner, relieved.

They went out of the alley. The droll teller picked at his finger-nails, which had a layer of something growing under them. It was moss, or maybe algae, wet and dark green. He'd had it under his nails for about fifty years but he was sure it was getting worse. He tried to dig it out but it stayed fixed.

'Isn't this where we just came from?' the man asked.

The droll teller looked around. He'd taken them back past the first meeting point. The harbour wall was in front of them, a steam boat on the horizon. 'This is the route,' he said.

The man and the woman glanced at each other once, shrugged. They weren't holding hands. They didn't walk next to each other; they left a gap, as if they were making room for someone else. The droll teller used to be able to see exactly who the lost person was, standing in the empty spaces people left for them. This time he hardly noticed.

They were walking up a long, residential street. The town had spread back from the harbour; the roads got wider and the houses got bigger. Reuben Gray, who was out messing with his car, called to the droll teller as they passed, but the droll teller didn't turn around. He pretended not to have heard. He didn't want anyone to give him away and a lot of people lacked subtlety. He'd known Reuben's grandfather: he'd been the first person in the town to own a car. He and the droll teller had rolled down the cliff in it, and crawled out of the window with one broken finger each. Reuben's grandfather said that only two events flashed through his mind as he was rolling, and they weren't the ones he was expecting. He wouldn't say what they were. For the droll teller there had been none at all, only a sudden stillness and quiet.

The woman looked at her watch and then announced, 'She should have landed by now.'

Her husband nodded. 'She will have landed.'

The woman looked at the droll teller. 'Our daughter, Lily,' she said, as if he had asked. 'She's gone off teaching and backpacking in Indonesia.'

'My wife thinks it's dangerous,' the man said. 'It's not dangerous.'

'For a year,' she said. 'A whole year.'

'Everyone's doing it now,' he said. 'It's not dangerous.'

Their voices spilled out suddenly, falling into an old argument.

'You're more likely to be killed by a donkey than in a plane crash,' the droll teller said. Something Harry had told him. He stopped and looked at a small scrap of wasteland behind the houses. There was a 'land for sale' sign up, a huge gull perched on top. Gulls would steal anything off you if you weren't careful. The earth was trampled and there were nettles and sloes at the edges. He could taste rust and flint, could feel something sharp digging in behind his shoulders, some old, distant pain, maybe not even his own. He tried to dredge something up but there was nothing.

The couple hovered behind him, looking where he was looking, expecting to be told something. They scoured the ground for clues. There was a heavy silence between them now. The man lifted his arm up, as if to touch his wife's back, let it drop. He put his hand in his pocket, looked at his wife's back.

'Nothing here,' the droll teller said. He trudged ahead, feeling an immense tiredness. He wanted a long rest, to lie down somewhere very quiet. He could still taste rust, like blood in his mouth. The sharp pain nestled in between his shoulders. Not his pain; he didn't want it. He tried to shake it off.

Since when had there been so many houses? All these houses and streets seemed to have appeared overnight, hundreds of them. The droll teller tried to picture what had been there before but he couldn't do it. Things had happened there, before the houses were built. He had been at the very centre – now where was he? He skirted the edges of the development, trying to find a way through, guessing each turning before he found the small town square and knew where he was again.

There was a statue of a man on a horse in the middle. The droll teller hadn't been into the square for a long time. The shops had changed round. No more blacksmiths. No more video shop – Mick had disappeared. He'd heard that Mick had last been seen wading out into the sea, although someone else had said he'd moved to another town with cheaper rents. There was a Chinese takeaway by the hardware store. The droll teller had a huge craving for Chinese takeaway – fried rice, sweet and sour sauce, the kind that made your heartbeat change its rhythm. He also craved the cider they used to sell on the stalls around the square, and that stew, so thick you could almost cut it, and older tastes that he could barely remember – saffron maybe, or another, richer spice that you couldn't get hold of any more.

The couple went up to the statue and looked at it, walked all the way round. The statue commemorated a local soldier who had fought in the Napoleonic Wars and been made a general. The thing was, the droll teller had met the man and he had been a real arse so he didn't want to talk about him. He had a cruel face, you could see it there in the bronze.

He ignored the statue and glanced around the square. He used to wake up there a lot after heavy nights, with people walking past him as they went between stalls and shops. They used to move him into the shade while he slept, but as years passed, no one moved him, and his face would blister in the sun.

A leaf skidded past him, and then another, and then the droll teller saw more leaves piled up in drifts. They were oak leaves, turned copper, from an oak that used to stand in the middle of the square. He looked away and when he looked back the leaves had gone. He thought he could smell gas lamps and hear the hiss of them. Over there: a small hand waving out of the pub window; over there: a man in a black coat, handcuffed, howling like a storm wind. He could hear the storm wind and the howling, and it took him a few seconds to realise that it was still the same quiet, clear day it had been before.

'A man howling,' he said.

'What was that?' the man asked, coming over. 'Sorry, we weren't ready.'

The droll teller bent over a deep chip in the wall of the butcher's, felt the rough edges. 'Look,' he said.

'What's that? A bullet hole?'

'A bullet hole,' he said. It probably was a bullet hole, or maybe a truck had clipped it. 'Yes. Bullets. Smugglers. Whisky, leather, chocolate. The town was poor, full of poor men, and it was extra money. The leader of the gang was a brutal man. His name was,' he paused for a second – the name was a blank. They'd want to know it. The butcher's family name was Bickle, it was up there on the sign, but hopefully they wouldn't notice. Bickle's daughter owned the shop now. He'd known the grandmother, and the one before that – maybe he'd been in love with one of them. He'd known his share of women, love came and went. 'Bickle,' he said. 'Harry Bickle. One dark and stormy night, something happened.' It had been a dark and stormy

216

night in the last story, but sod it. 'A gunfight. Shots missed and hit the wall.'

The woman nodded, smiling, expecting more.

'They hit the wall,' the droll teller said again and pointed at the mark. A group of geese caught his eye and he looked up and watched them. It sounded like their wings were creaking. He watched the geese flying over. The couple looked up and watched them too.

'Can you remember that time all those geese landed in our garden?' the woman asked her husband. 'There were about ten of them. They just landed there for a couple of minutes and then at the same time they all looked up and flew away again. They just lifted up.'

'I don't remember that,' he said.

'You were there.'

'I don't think I was there.'

'You were standing right there. It was before Lily. We watched them out of the window. You said they looked like they were wearing stockings over their heads, like they were going to hold up a bank.'

'Are you sure I said that?' he asked.

'You said that,' she replied quietly. 'But it doesn't matter.'

They were all still looking up at the sky even though the geese had passed. The droll teller used to feel himself swooping in with the geese, seeing the map of the land from their eyes – he'd known every bump and curve of it. He watched the empty sky, remembered that a man had once looked up for so long his neck had locked and he had to look up for ever. He looked down again and rubbed his aching neck.

'Better get to the mines,' he said. It would all be over soon. He would mash something together on the way up, spin them something, then he could find Harry and go to Meg's. The night would pass easily at least. He reached into his pocket, checked the money was still there.

They went through the square, back through streets with houses on either side, maybe the same ones as before, maybe not.

'Do you, I mean, are we going the right way?' the man asked. 'Aren't we going to end up at the harbour again?'

The droll teller nodded. 'Forwards and back again,' he said.

Reuben Gray was ahead, still out with his car. He was whistling something; he had a loud, beautiful whistle that travelled miles.

'Wait here,' the droll teller said. He walked ahead to talk to Reuben, find out the way to the mines.

'Did you blank me earlier?' Reuben asked.

'Sort of,' the droll teller said. 'The mines. Are they right at the harbour, or left?'

'Left,' Reuben said. 'It's a hike. Steep. You hit those hundred steps before you get there.' He reached into the bonnet and wiped a dirty cloth around.

'Hundred steps?'

'Who are those people you're with?'

'Giving them a tour. It's good money.'

Reuben nodded. 'That other tour has a minibus to get up there. It needs work. I said I'd sort out the clutch but he hasn't got back to me.'

'A minibus.'

'Yeah. The clutch is screwed on it.'

'I'll give you a fiver for a lift up,' the droll teller said. He felt bitter parting with five out of the twenty, but it was going to be a long, steep walk otherwise.

'I can't,' Reuben told him. 'My car's knackered.' There was a bumper sticker on it that said, 'I'm only speeding because I need to take a dump.' The doors were rusty and peeling. His whistle followed the droll teller down the road.

'We might go over the hour,' the droll teller said when he got back to the couple.

'Don't worry about it,' the woman said. 'No hurry.'

'How much over?' the man asked at the same time, his voice trailing off like vapour at the end.

Left at the harbour, across a stony beach, up along the path. The hundred steps were there in the distance, a thin snake coiling up the cliff. The droll teller hadn't walked this far in a long time. He had a stitch but he trudged on, one foot in front of the other.

The landscape was low, dreary, windblown. Gorse bush followed gorse bush, stone followed stone. The droll teller kept stopping to make sure he was heading towards the steps. He used to be able to locate exactly where he was, used to be able to move from place to place, town to town, without even thinking about it. The stories were embedded in the landscape and he followed them, from that cove to that hill to that ruin – it was all mapped out. When he looked around him now, he saw only flickers: in that stone shaped like a giant table, in that gnarled tree, nothing more than flickers. The grass and the sea stretched out in all directions. It was as if he had spilled water over a map and the lines had blurred and shifted into each other.

'I didn't know it would be this far,' the woman said. She ran a hand over her face, unwrapped her thin scarf. 'Are we almost there?'

'At the top,' the droll teller said. He pointed up the steps, which were carved into the cliff, centuries old, part earth and wood, part concrete, part stone.

'Up there?' the man asked. His hair had been pulled out of shape by the wind and was all knots and twists.

They started climbing. The droll teller took each step carefully, hoisting his weight up slowly. The steps were uneven, and he stumbled once or twice, caught himself. As he walked, he started to feel that he knew the shape of the next step before he took it. Halfway up, he was finding a firm hold every time. On one step: a faint footprint in the concrete that exactly fitted his own, the cross-hatch of his boot tread.

The engine houses loomed over. When they reached the top, the couple stopped to gulp in air. The droll teller wanted to keep walking, although the stitch was tearing through his side and into his ribs and his breathing had turned to gasping. He went through the empty car park, across the grass and the rocks and the thrift. The mining buildings were scattered all around: chimneys, engine houses, pump houses, old frameworks. At first, it looked like a place that was still active, that was filled with voices and work, but then there was the stillness, and the quiet and the fallen bricks.

There were two more engine houses further down the cliff, perched on the edge like seabirds' nests. There was a strong wind. It hit the droll teller full in the face and it felt good – it reminded him of the times when, after a long story, he would escape the heat and the smoke to stand slap bang in the night, lifting his face up to the moon and the stars.

A voice and the muffled boom of a church bell worked their way through the wind towards him. He stood still, listening. The bell tolled again, quiet and muffled. The line 'A man had a premonition' went round and round his head but he didn't know the end of the sentence.

He looked over the edge. The rocks down there were like teeth. The water broke itself apart on them, turning into foam and spray. There was a ship down there, leaning on the rocks. It hadn't been there before, but the droll teller saw it now: it appeared suddenly and clearly. He could hear the boards creaking as it rose and fell in the tide. He could hear people shouting. It was a bad wreck, and among the crates and boxes there were bodies washing up on to the sand.

'Annie Jones,' the droll teller muttered. 'Jamie Jones.'

'What was that?' the man asked, coming closer. He beckoned to his wife.

'Seamus Morley, Peter Trelawney.' The names came back to the droll teller easily. 'Thomas Chapel, Toby O'Sullivan.' He saw each of the bodies and he saw the crates spilling out hundreds of oranges on to the sand. Everyone in the town had eaten oranges for weeks after, it was the first time anyone had ever tried them. He could taste their sweet sharpness and feel the juice on his lips and fingers.

He looked away, and when he looked back the ship was still there, creaking and groaning.

'Spain,' he said to the couple. 'It came from Spain.'

He told them about the wreck, about the creaking boards, about how it had been a dark, still night – so still that no one knew how the ship had found itself on rocks. He told them about the bodies and the oranges. He tried to describe the taste of the oranges – how sweet they were, how he was tasting them again now. He could feel his drenched clothes and skin as he hauled bodies on to the beach, his arms almost yanked right out of their sockets. There was no story yet – it was just a taste, just the feeling of soaking, heavy clothes. He realised he was muttering it all, muttering and speaking too fast, trying to get all the details in, trying to make them see the actual ship, the image of it right down there now, on the rocks.

'Never mind,' he said. 'Never mind. Over here.' There was more.

There were more images and memories just out of reach, half-glimpsed and crowding in.

He moved towards the railway tracks which cut across the site, and followed one until it disappeared into a mine shaft. The shaft was steep and black and impossible to see down into.

'They go under the sea,' the droll teller said. He remembered a tunnel under the water, small and tight like an artery, the drumbeat of waves.

The woman shivered. 'Think how dark it would be,' she said.

'The water would sound like a heart,' her husband said suddenly.

She looked at him and nodded, then reached up to tidy his knotted hair.

The droll teller could hear something in the mine, something knocking, something moving around deep inside it. He thought it could be one of the mine spirits, shuffling, going about its slow business. Mine spirits were pale and blind-eyed, sensitive to light. They would find tin for the miners if the price was right. They were hunched and sleepy and weak-kneed but could smell tin or copper through solid earth from miles away. Was that what the story was about? Mine spirits? A man had a premonition. What was that bell doing, tolling quietly in the back of his mind?

He sat down on the grass and waited. The ground felt good, it was good to sit down – the grass was springy and there was thrift and clover tangled in it. The couple sat down next to him and waited. They wrapped their coats tighter. They sat quiet and still. The engine houses stood over them and it seemed that, at any moment, smoke would start pouring out of the chimneys again.

No sound except the waves and then geese, as another skein flew over.

The tapping started again and got louder. It sounded to the droll teller as if something was climbing up out of the mine. His senses sharpened, knitted together. It could be a deep tapping, or it could be that bell, tolling. Was the bell in the mine or in the sea? He remembered a bell sunk in a shipwreck that still tolled underwater. A man had a premonition. Tap, tap. And then there was shuffling, movement. He could hear the story creeping out of the mine towards him. It was backing out slowly, hauling itself out bit by bit. It was taking its time. There were waves. There was a train carriage. There was a lamp swinging in the dark. The bell tolled louder and now here he was beginning again; somehow, despite everything, he was beginning again.

# Acknowledgements

Thank you to my agent Elizabeth Sheinkman and my editor Jenna Johnson; thank you to everyone at Houghton Mifflin Harcourt; Sam North, Philip Hensher and Andy Brown at the Centre for Creative Writing and Arts, University of Exeter; Michel and Eva Faber; Guy Bower; Emma Bird; and Ben Smith for his endless encouragement and support.

Grateful acknowledgement is also due to the Arts and Humanities Research Council for funding my MA in Creative Writing, where this collection of stories began.

## A NOTE ON THE AUTHOR

Lucy Wood has a Master's degree in Creative Writing from Exeter University. She grew up in Cornwall. *Diving Belles* is her first work.

A NOTE ON THE TYPE

The text of this book is set in Adobe Garamond. It is one of several versions of Garamond based on the designs of Claude Garamond. It is thought that Garamond based his font on Bembo, cut in 1495 by Francesco Griffo in collaboration with the Italian printer Aldus Manutius. Garamond types were first used in books printed in Paris around 1532. Many of the present-day versions of this type are based on the *Typi Academiae* of Jean Jannon cut in Sedan in 1615.

Claude Garamond was born in Paris in 1480. He learned how to cut type from his father and by the age of fifteen he was able to fashion steel punches the size of a pica with great precision. At the age of sixty he was commissioned by King Francis I to design a Greek alphabet, for this he was given the honourable title of royal type founder. He died in 1561.